Leprechaun Legacy

Chuck Bowers

iUniverse, Inc.
New York   Bloomington

Leprechaun Legacy

Copyright © 2009 Chuck Bowers

This is a work of fiction. All of the characters,
names, incidents, organizations, and dialogue in
this novel are either the products of the author's
imagination or are used fictitiously.

iUniverse books may be ordered through
booksellers or by contacting:

iUniverse
1663 Liberty Drive
Bloomington, IN 47403
www.iuniverse.com
1-800-Authors (1-800-288-4677)

Because of the dynamic nature of the Internet, any Web
addresses or links contained in this book may have changed
since publication and may no longer be valid. The views
expressed in this work are solely those of the author and do
not necessarily reflect the views of the publisher, and the
publisher hereby disclaims any responsibility for them.

ISBN: 978-1-4401-2248-4 (pbk)
ISBN: 978-1-4401-2249-1 (ebk)

Printed in the United States of America

iUniverse rev. date: 2/25/2009

This book is dedicated to my children
Brad – Jessica – Charlie – Leroy
Also to Cody Martin

*May they always have wonderful dreams and the courage
to fulfill them?*

With love and heart filled appreciation to my Mother
Alma Jean Henderson, for her Friendship, never-ending
love for her children, and her encouragement to
complete this work. Which otherwise could not have
been born.

A Special Thank You to all my friends and supporters
for helping make one of my dreams come true.

Forward

This book was written for the young at heart, for readers 9 to 90 who love their imagination and dreams. The story is one version of how the mischievous leprechauns came to exist. It's a tale of a young Irish boy who through accident, comes to live in a fairytale world that comes to life.

This story is of adventure, friendship, love, war, Kings, Knights, and some very ugly creatures. If you like to daydream you'll enjoy the pages that follow. So find a quite place, sit back, relax and take the adventure.

CONTENTS

CHAPTER 1
THE MCNAIRE CLAN

Have you ever wondered what it would be like to live in a land where magic and fairy tales are as real as the sun and the moon? Hundreds of years of tradition leave one with the sense of reality. This tale involves a boy from a typical Irish farming family, but wait, this tale is more than typical.

First, we have Grandfather McNaire, The Elder of The Northern McNaire Clan' his son Michael, and Michael's wife Jean, their children, Thomas the oldest, Susan the oldest daughter, Alexander the youngest son, and Sharon Lee, the youngest.

The McNaires as all previous northern clansmen, which date back to the Holy Wars, were potato farmers.

This lifestyle involved long, hot summers and sparse, cold winters.

Grandfather spent most of his time at the White Horse Inn since his beloved wife passed away. Thomas, Sue, and Alex, would wait up for Grandfathers return home from the White Horse Inn. The old man would spin a yarn about the magical leprechauns and their mystical pots of gold, or sing an old Irish ballad, to tickle the fancy of the children as his elders did for him when he was a young buck. Be it myth, legend, or just plain blarney, the elusive elves, pixies, and leprechauns, were still ranked highest in tale telling.

One spring evening the McNaires dined out, as they chose to call eating their evening meal outside under a giant elderberry tree. This is where our story begins.

"Thomas, I want you and Alex up at dawn, dressed, fed, and in the East field by half past six." Said Michael. "Yes, Sir! And father would you please inform Alexander he must plant more than three rows to my seven." replied Thomas.

"My word" injected Grandfather. "Three rows to seven, perhaps Thomas is in ranks for a ribbon. Three rows sounds a fair days' labor for a lad". It was normal for the old man to favor Alex over the others. Seemed he admired what the rest looked down on as daydreaming or dilly-dallying as Sharon Lee would call it. "Never you mind father". Snapped Michael. "Those fields will take the three of us most of the spring to plant. The eye-potatoes are already sprouting. We've only a week to ten days on the outside". "Sue, you and Sharon help your mother prepare for the Founders Day Carnival this weekend". Finished Michael. That order, began broken conversation around the table until dinners' end.

"Take a pipe with me papa?" Michael asked his father. "Sure thing Mike", answered Grandfather McNaire. "Father, I've been meaning to talk to you about Alex. It seems you side with him a might more than the other children. His chores at home aren't the only areas he's slack in, his schoolwork also needs a leg up. It seems he has his mind elsewhere. I'm beginning to wonder if he might need special help." Michael stated, with real concern in his voice. " Michael, Leave the boy to grow. As I remember, your mind would wander about when you were his age." Grandfather said with a smile breaking across his lips. "Maybe papa, maybe." said Mike.

Next morning as the sun kissed the crest of the blue-mountains beyond the McNaire farm, Thomas and Alex were off to the fields. The oxen cart full of quarter-eyed potatoes creaked as they rolled onto the dirt road.

"Alex, I'm sorry about what I said at dinner and all. It's just that I'm getting tired of carrying your load and mine." Thomas said not wanting to hurt Alexs' feelings.

"I'll try harder Thomas. Sure don't want to let father down after the winter we had." Alex stated.

Meanwhile, Jean and the girls began the morning chores. What a loathsome job it was, with pigs to slop, chickens to feed, and cows to milk. Then came their favorite thing to do. As a tradition Irish mothers gave instruction to their daughters in the art of cooking and baking. Usually accompanied by a lot of gossip. The lessons always produced a bounty of cupcakes, pies, mostly rhubarb pie, Grandfathers' favorite. Also, mothers special sweet cherry tarts. Besides entering them in the baking contest, there were always enough left over for the dinner table, as well as a few to be eaten while making them. Mother McNaire directed a question toward Sue. "Are you planning to attend the dance Saturday night?" Asked Jean. "Hopefully I'll be going, it just depends." blushed Sue. "Ya, depends on Brad O'Shey, I'll bet," cut in Sharon Lee. Followed by, "Sue has a boyfriend. Sue has a boyfriend." "Mother, make her stop." Begged Sue. "That's enough, both of you." came a voice from the living-room, as Mike entered the kitchen. "Don't!" Began Jean. Ka-boom! The screen door slammed. "Slam the screen door, Michael." Finished, Jean. "Too late love, I'll have to fix the spring on it sometime." Jested Mike. "Sure you will Mr. McNaire, as you always say." Laughed Jean. "Girls, comfort your dear poor mother till I return from the long, dirty," … began Michel. "Oh be off with ya Mike before the day's spent and your sons wonder what's happened to ya." Interrupted Jean.

Thomas and Alex had the cart unloaded and had already begun their work when Mike pulled up. Mike gave a shout to each of them to let them know he was heading into the village to take care of business.

He generally stopped at the White Horse Inn, to catch up on local news. Also to see if anything new was to be learned from the travelers that stopped, as they went about their journeys.

Back at the fields the boys were working. The heat from the noon sun hit the fields, driving the boys to seek relief in the cool shade of trees. Alex headed for his favorite tree and propped his back up against it. Soon he was nodding off, as sleep began to take over, Alex noticed a quick movement in the grass in front of him. Thinking nothing of it he began to nod off again. Then another movement caught his attention. No longer sleepy, he focused on the spot where he had last noticed the movement. No? It couldn't be true, as he rubbed his eyes. He thought he had seen a twinkle from a buckle on a green hat worn by a tiny man.

Alex was about to yell out to his brother, when he thought better of it. Thinking his imagination had gotten the better of him, he dismissed the event and soon fell back to sleep.

He awoke to hear Thomas say. "Come along Alex, let's call it a day and head home." As Alex stood up, he decided not to tell Thomas about what he thought he'd seen. Thomas would have probably thought him bonkers.

As the day slowly passed on, one by one the family showed up at home. The boys tired, the girls buzzing like bees, mom on the front porch working on her needlepoint. They all stopped to listen as grandfather came down the road loudly singing an old Irish song. Father, back from town, was sitting at his desk finishing up the days' figures. After dinner Alex went to the barn to bed down the animals. He then climbed into the hayloft to gaze at the clouds in the night sky as the light of the moon silhouetted them. He began to think about the after-noon events. Over and over he replayed the picture of what he thought he'd seen. It now began to worry him. As he went to bed later that night, his sleep was troubled with thoughts of the little man and his tiny green hat.

Alex sprung up and bolted out of his bed the next morning. Which surprised everyone. Alex rarely, moved that quickly except on Christmas morning or Easter Sunday. In the fields that day Alex worked hard, trying to keep his mind on what he was doing. When noon approached he sought out his favorite tree. As he sat against it he fought the sleep he felt coming on. A restless night and working hard in the field were too much, and he fell fast asleep dreaming of the little man.

The sound of the triangle clanging woke him. It was time to head back home for dinner. He hurried down the road catching up with Thomas, who hadn't noticed that he had been asleep most of the afternoon. It was Friday and the smell of freshwater perch filtered through the air. Fish was not one of Alex favorite foods. He would smother it with lots of lemon juice. After Dinner the family met in the living room to talk about the Founders Day Picnic and to take a last minute inventory. Founders Day was a very festive event. Though it came once a year, the re-enactment of the finding of their village was always colorful. A small circus and carnival occupied the young and of course good food, conversation, met the needs of the adults.

Grandfather and the other heads of clans-men would dress in the traditional Irish attire. Bagpipes filled the lakeside with sounds of beautiful Irish melodies strong with tradition and mellow with age.

Mike and several of the younger men would have tests of strength and skill at the pole throw. Thomas and Alex doing the shot-put and discus. Sue and Sharon-Lee entered the baking and arts-crafts contests. It was custom, a lass of Sues' age would raffle off a basket lunch to share with a lucky lad. There was no secret, about Sue wanting Brad to win hers. Brad O'Shey had courted the McNaire lass for several months now and it had been said that they would marry the following summer. As tradition they needed and had the permission and blessings of their elders.

Saturday morning came and the days' events seemed to flash by quickly. Clan reunions were always large. There were aunts, uncles, 1st, 2nd, 3rd cousins right down the line. Large families were common and regarded as necessary for survival of the clans on the Emerald Isle.

As shadows grew longer, and evening began to steal the light of day, Sharon fell asleep on her mothers shoulder. Face sticky from cotton-candy and her hands wrapped tightly around her favorite doll Chelsea. Sue hurried to find the O'Shey clan, wanting to be present to give Brad the chance to ask her to the dance by the lake shore. Grandfather and Mike joined the other men around the Central Bonfire located in the Dell. The woman began the process of clearing and cleaning tables while the young ones began to fall asleep. Thomas and most of the boys his age were still playing hide and seek while Alex chose to walk along the far side of the lake, to see how many constellations he could count among the millions of stars in the clear evening sky.

It was around midnight when Thomas and Sue came along, followed by Alex.

They all climbed into the buckboard for the trip back home. Being lovers of nature, they enjoyed the scenic route along the lake back to their house. It was in the wee hours of the morning when the stock was finally fed, and bedded down.

CHAPTER 2
THE RUNAWAY TART

Alex finished his daily chores and was pardoned to do what he enjoyed most, knapping under the shade tree beside the fields. He fixed a small jug of lemonade and two tarts for his long journey. As he rambled his way along toward the fields, he began to day dream about his seeing, or at least what he thought he had seen, what could have only been a wee people, as folks in that part of Ireland called them, more generally known as Leprechauns. I'm alone he thought and I can think, as I like. As he came upon his spot beneath the tree he began to chuckle to himself. To entertain such blarney tickled him.

After he had eaten one tart and drank a glass of lemonade, he leaned back and propped his back up against the trunk of the large tree. He often wondered about foreign places and what it would be like to have lived in the time of knights, kings, and dragons. He began to daydream of these things when his attention was drawn to the remaining cherry tart. It was turned on its' side. Not knowing if he had placed it as such, he began to ponder; Hmm, did I do that? I must have, he thought. Placing it bottom to top he returned to his daydream.

As the sun climbed, the shadows drew short. Alex, lost in his imaginative time, hadn't noticed the tart was again on its' side but this time it seemed to have grown legs. He began hearing short, shrill squeaks. A field mouse he thought. The sound came from the same place each time. Then he noticed his runaway tart. It was top to bottom now and not at all near where he had placed it earlier. It was a few meters away, the same place the awful squeaks came from. As Alex leaned over to retrieve his snack, he caught sight of the tiny green hat with the shiny buckle. After rubbing his eyes several times, it still remained. It appeared the tart had also sprung a head. Alex, now on his knees, ever so slowly took a closer look. The tart began shaking and the squeaks became louder. As he came as close as he dared, the noise cleared some. He thought he could make out the call for help. As he lifted the tart, the squeals ceased. He froze in his position and squeezed the tart so tight that the filling jetted out, through the air and covered what was already a very frustrated and angry leprechaun!

The wee person stared at Alex with flames in his eyes. "I'd be off in a twinkle if what I tried to steal from you, wasn't covering me from me cap to me boots." Snapped the leprechaun. Alex jaw dropped. "I've caught a leprechaun." Shouted Alex. Each time he said it his eyes grew wider. "Now see here lad. I'll be thanking ya for saving me hide, but it was I what caught me-self. Embarrassing, yes, and I'll be asking ya for a kerchief and some water. If ya hadn't made me pick it up twice, I'd be belly full and on me way." Frowned the leprechaun. "See hear, little man, it was your doings to pick it up to begin with." Said Alex. "Yes, yes, so it was," replied the wee person.

Alex gave him his hankie then made an error. He left the leprechaun and went to the creek for water. He went ever so quickly but not quickly enough. When he returned, all that was left was a few crumbs. Alex searched and searched, calling, come out, "come out leprechaun. Show yourself." Of course, there came no reply. Alex gave up as the shadows grew. He sat back down under the tree and this time he didn't try to talk himself out of it. It was a fact. He had seen a wee man about 22cm high, hat, buckle, beard, and all. He sighed in relief. "I'm glad no one was around to hear me searching for the rodent." He said out loud as he collected his jug and headed home. All evening he planned different ways to catch the mischievous creature. That, being the only way anyone would believe his story of a tart bandit dressed in a green suit. He tossed all night without deep sleep. As the rooster crowed, he rolled out of his bunk.

Michael, Thomas, Jean, and the girls were sitting at the breakfast table as Alex tore through the kitchen. "Alex! Alex! Slow up." Yelled Thomas. "You'd have us believe the devil himself was after ya." "What is the hurry?" Said Thomas. "I need some things from the barn." Answered Alex. "What kinds of things?" Questioned Michael. "A grindstone and gloves, to sharpen me hoe, Papa." Replied Alex. "Here now, ya sit yourself to the table. The stone and all can wait till you've finished eating." Ordered Michael. "Yes Papa," replied Alex. "Mother, would there be any tarts left over?" "I would like one in my lunch today if there is!" Finished Alex. "Of course, Alex, is there any other request for lunch before we've finished our morning meal?" Jested Jean.

As Michael and the boys left the house, the girls gathered the dishes and the gossip soon began their day. Summer vacation for the farmer meant no school, less play, and more work. The McNaire children were well behaved and not accustomed to complaining. However, it wasn't like Alex to be anxious to hit the fields. "Get the things you need from the barn son and I'll drop you and your brother off on me way to the village." Stated Michael.

While in the barn, Alex cut a length of bailing twine and rolled it into a ball then stuffed it into his coveralls. Next, he picked up a sharpening stone and a pair of cloth gloves. He looked around until he found a small wooden crate used for odds and ends. He put the gloves and sharpening stone into the crate and then hurried to the wagon.

Michael told the boys that they were doing a good job in the East field and that he wanted them to finish up where they were. He wanted to plow the North end of the land towards the weeks end. After final instructions, Alex and Thomas jumped off the wagon, running along side to snare, their lunches and tools. "Take care not to work your selves too hard in the heat of the day." said Michael, as he snapped the reigns and headed his rig towards the village.

"Alex, there are twenty-three rows left to hill. I'll start at the far side of the field and you start where you left off Friday. We'll work until we meet each other. Let's try to finish before the end of the week. That will give us an extra day or so to finish quartering the eyed potatoes." Said Thomas. "Sure, Thomas, it's better working in the shade of the barn than out here in the sun." Replied Alex. Thomas headed for the far side of the field while Alex placed his box beside his favorite tree. He took the stone out of the box and struck the edge of the hoe hard enough for his brother to hear the blade of the hoe ring out. Alex repeated this until Thomas was out of sight.

Now Alex began to put his plan together. He took his lunch pale and opened it to take out the cherry tart his mom had packed for him. "God bless you mama." Alex said in a whisper. He placed the tart in the place where he thought the stolen tart had been. Sitting the box on end, he sat it beside the bait of his trap, tied the hemp string around a twig. Then slowly lowered the box until the edge of the box rested on the twig. He giggled to himself as he unrolled the twine, until he was behind the big trees trunk. To test his brilliant scheme he yanked on the string, pulling the twig out from under the box and his trap was sprung. The box covered the tart and anything else that might be under it.

He left the box down and whistled his way to the mounds, neatly piled one by one down long rows. He looked for Thomas but all he could see of him was the top of his head as it bounced to and fro. Alex himself worked hard and much faster than usual. The sun rose high and hot until the shadows were almost gone. Soon it was time for lunch and for his plan to be put into action. He hurried from his labor and re-set the trap. He gulped down some lemonade and quickly ate his lunch. Always keeping an eye on the cherry tart under the box.

Time seemed to drag on until the sun cast shadows again, on the downward end of the day. Disappointed and tired from the hard work that morning Alex jerked the string and he heard the box plop to the ground.

Mumbling to himself, he went back to work thinking of new ways to catch the leprechaun. He tried to whistle and even sing to get his mind back on work. He wondered about; how many is there, is there more than one, could he catch the wee man, and is there really a pot of gold? Finally thinking of all the things his family could do with a pot of gold. Seemed to make his day go by faster.

Thomas singing brought Alex around from his daydreams of fame and fortune. He noticed his brother from across the field heading in his direction. Alex turned toward his tree, grabbed his hoe and sack and ran to undo his trap. Before Thomas could see it and ask too many questions. When Alex got to his trap, he dropped what he was carrying, wound the string up, threw off the twig, lifted the box and froze. The cherry tart was gone. Not only was the tart gone but in its place was the hankie Alex had given to the leprechaun. Alex began to question himself, how in the world? "How in the world, what?" ask Thomas, coming up behind him. "Ah, nothing, just my kerchief, I must of dropped it," said Alex. "Yes, that would explain what it's doing on the ground under a box." Said Thomas. "Pick it up and let's go." About that time the triangle began to clang. Thomas told Alex that they had gotten a lot done that day. All Alex could do was hang his head and murmur, Yes, a lot, if you only knew how much.

Michael and grandfather McNaire talked mostly about the weather, as the family ate that night. If the rains didn't start soon the crops would turn to dust. Thomas and Sharon Lee were making faces at one another over the hominy they both ate out of respect for Jean. They both hated the taste of it. Jean and Susan were talking at the same time but both managed to end with the same sentence. Alex couldn't have cared less. He sat with his eyes wide open and not hearing a single thing, just stared into space.

After dinner, Michael and Grandfather took their pipes, as was their habit. The girls and mother went off to do chores. Thomas and Alex to feed and bed down the animals. Finally, Alex climbed into the hayloft to ponder and daydream.

CHAPTER 3
THE STORM

Alex searched the sky until his gaze rested on the bright flicker of Venus, a short drop and to the right of the moon in the Emerald Island skies. Alexs' imagination painted boyish images of a strange culture of a three eyed, short and plump society living on the planet. After what seemed like hours, Alex yawned as his thoughts came back to earth. He began to climb out of the hayloft. His thoughts turned to the leprechaun and it's smug trick of leaving the kerchief under the trap. Alex became frustrated and tried to think only positive thoughts. Reassured he would catch the mischievous creature. Alex went to bed. He tossed all night, his mind unable to free itself from the days' events in the field. Alex was slow in rolling out of bed the next morning. He felt more tired than when he had first tried to sleep.

By the time the family was up and ready for a new day, the sun was burning hot. As the boys and Michael rode toward the field, they could see stretched out in front of them waves of heat. It looked like a giant lake. "Thomas and Alex, work only till noon then break until it's cooled off. Then we'll work until dusk. This might be the way of it till the plowing is done. I'll bring you cold drinks on me way from the village." Said Michael. As Michael pulled up to the Mercantile, the dust from the street settled on the seat of the buckboard. He took his cap off and wiped his brow.

"Tis, a dry burner of a day Michael McNaire." He whispered to himself. "Took to talking to yourself have ya son?" Heard Michael as he looked up to see Squire O'Connor, the constable.   "I." Said Michael, "Take a stein of ale, would ya Squire?" "Sure would lad, as soon as I've finished at the county seat, I will." Answered the Squire "Be on your way then, I'll see to the latest prices of things and meet up with ya at the White Horse." Said Michael. After Michael had studied the market, he left the mercantile and headed for the edge of town toward the White Horse Inn. The air was thick and hard to breath. He passed through the swinging doors. The hinges squeaked as he entered. It was around the hour of ten as he leaned up to the rail. The Inn was fairly active, as it is in the summer months. Grandfather gave Michael a nod from across the one long room. There were sleeping rooms that skirted three sides of the White Horse. At this time of year they were usually full of travelers headed for Dubland. Grandfather McNaire finished his game of chess and then nestled to the counter next to his son. "Michael," greeted grandfather. "Did you put the lads on split day shifts?" "I," Said Michael, "and told them to hide in during the heat of the day. I'll drop them a cold drink on me way back." "Good, son," said grandfather. Squire interrupted the two and gestured for them to join him at a table. He ordered three schooners of cold ale and began his usual run down of the village. He was a large man with leather tough skin. His laugh was deep and throaty. The three men drank and passed the time in leisure. "Pat," yelled Squire, "three more steins." "Hold up on one of those Patrick, and wrap two iced orange drinks for me boys." Said Michael as he dismissed himself from the company and took to the road back to his farm. The heat was stifling hot and Alex told Michael. "I think I'll dally here awhile Papa, take a swim, and be home in an hour or so." "As ya wish." said Michael. Thomas hopped aboard the buckboard and seated himself beside his father. The horse pulled out and headed down the road.

Alex immediately retrieved his box and twine from where he had placed them in the berry bushes by his tree. He set the trap. Not having a tart for bait, he placed his kerchief under the box wrapped around a stone. Hoping the wee mans' curiosity would bring him near enough to catch. He laid himself behind the trunk of his tree and dropped the twine over its' bark. Michael and Thomas hadn't been gone more than fifteen minutes when the first cool breeze swept over the fields and hit Alex bare shoulders. They were still moist from swimming in the creek near the fields. The breeze chilled, but not enough to concern the lad. He was pre-occupied with catching a leprechaun. Only moments later a second and much healthier breeze snapped Alex to his feet. He looked at the sky, which was clear as blue glass. No indication of where the cool wind came from.

While at the home steed, Michael and Thomas had just finished unhitching the horse. Thomas was brushing the leather from the horse as Michael came out of the barn where he had hung the tack. Thomas felt the breeze and thought it very refreshing. However, Michael froze in his tracks. He had heard tales of cool winds on dry, hot days and his look was one of fear. His eyes searched the horizon. At first, he noticed nothing unusual about the endless blue sky. It was clear, so hot and blandly vacant. As he looked round about him, he noticed the stock fighting, and becoming excited. The goats and sheep began to nay and the cows to bellow. He could hear the horse whinny. Michael tried to remain calm as his eyes met those of Thomas. They simultaneously looked to the northern sky. The source of disturbance was instantly obvious. Clouds, like great waves upon the sea, were rolling and seemed to engulf themselves. They were folding inward then more ferociously outward. Making a darker and more sinister looking wave each time. The kitchen screen door blew out of Jeans' grasp as she stepped onto the porch of the house. She screamed for Michael. "In the name of Saint Peter, what is happening?" In a stern and frightened tone of voice, Michael began to shout out orders. The members of the family jumped to his commands trying not to let fear overpower his direction. "Thomas, set the horse free, let him run. Open the coral gates and let the cattle and sheep out." "Cut the nanny loose, Jean!

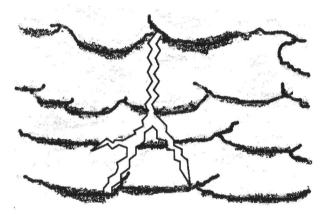

Yelled Michael. "Gather provisions and get the girls to the cellar. Hurry now. The storm will hit any second." Grandfather McNaire was being pushed down the path by the stiff wind that was steadily becoming stronger. He laughed out loud as if being tickled by it all. Everyone was busy and in such a fit it wasn't until Michael was pulling the cellar door to, he heard Sharon Lee scream for her doll, Chelsea. As Thomas volunteered to fetch it Michael snapped, "Stay put, all of you. I'll retrieve the doll." He gathered Chelsea and a pillow from Sharon- Lees' bed and vaulted through the kitchen door onto the porch. His attention was drawn to the barn. Directly behind the barn, a sheet of rain poured down, pulling a veil of black over the barn. Great bolts of lightening ripped the sky as the sounds of thunder shattered the windows. At his feet, pellets of rain hit the parched dirt of the yard and puffs of dust rose. He knew, at anytime, the force of the storm would engulf his farm. Slamming the cellar door behind him, he could feel the battering rain and hail hit the door. When he turned to his family in the flicker of the oil lamps, dread filled them all. Jean hysterically wrenched out, "Alex my baby!" "God help us! My baby is still out there." Grandfather and Thomas grabbed hold of Michael before he could reach the first stair leading to the outside. "The matter is in greater hands than ours now, Michael," said grandfather McNaire.

Alex, with his eyes still fixed on his trap, noticed the second breeze was chilly and damp. It was not at all in place for such a dry day. He decided it best to put his shirt and socks back on. After he stood up, he could hear a sound like a freight train. He finished putting on his shirt, thinking; good. It's rain and we need it. Then he looked about and the storm clouds told him it was more than just rain. Before he had his shoes and socks on he was drenched and took to the cover of his tree. It offered him little protection from the driving rains. The loud clasp of thunder scared him; it seemed too close. The sky lit up with veins of lightening. Alex, frightened, knew he was in danger. Great bolts of lightening tore through the clouds to find the earth of the fields. They are so close, ventured Alex. An arch of lightening blinded Alex. He heard the piercing crack as it split the tree, but he never heard the thunder that followed that bolt of lightening.

CHAPTER 4
A RUDE AWAKENING

Alex felt cold and clammy when he first came around. He tried to move but couldn't. His eyes sluggishly opened. He couldn't quite make out what he was seeing. He saw only gray and black shapes and figures. His ears seemed to be plugged and he could hardly determine the sounds about him. His mouth felt dry and he couldn't swallow. He struggled, but no matter how hard he tried, he couldn't yell out or move. After trying for what seemed like hours, his mind closed and he went back to sleep. The next time he awoke things were much more clear and the throbbing pain in his head was sharp. He rolled his eyes in every direction but all he could see was the roof of what appeared to be a cave. There were torches burning along the walls. He could hear the sound of marching from what must have been an army of a hundred pairs of feet. He tried to speak but found his mouth was gagged. When he tried to move he found his arms and legs were bound. Then a face appeared directly over his. It was the face of a tiny woman with a smile. She spoke to Alex in a soft rich tone. "Ah lad, you've come back to us." "Tis a good thing too. You had me doubting me nursing, ya did." Said the female.

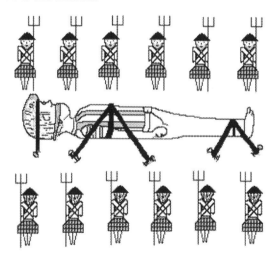

The grayness began to lift from Alex as he heard the woman shout. "Fetch the doctor and captain of the guard." When the two arrived the doctor starred into Alexs' eyes and began repeating himself. "Hmm, Hmm, and Hmmmm." "Well doc, what's the tally?" "Is the lad going to make it?" Ask the Captain. "Yes, of course he's going to make it," said the doctor. "Just the same I don't think you need rile the lad until he is stronger. Also, I'd have you remove the ropes and he'll need nourishment. For that he will need to eat." Added the doctor.

"Take the bonds and gag off." ordered the captain. Alex felt hands moving over, under and around him. "Easy now lad, can ya set up at all?" The nurse asked. Alex propped his head and back up while resting on his elbows. He gasped as he leaned up. He was in a huge cave surrounded by wee people. He felt like a giant. Which he might well have seemed to them, thought Alex. There were two rows of the small creatures on both sides of him. They each had a trident in one hand and the fist of the other on the hilt of a sword. They were dressed in leather kilts with cross straps holding them up. The straps were studded with colored stones. Most of the wee people had black onyx stones a few with red bloodstones. At the head of each row was one with a white opal and the captain had a mixture of all three with a large green emerald in the center where the straps crossed. "I'll leave him to you for the time being." "I have more urgent matters to attend to," said the captain. "I will leave some guards with you and I am to be summoned when the lad is strong enough to reason with." finished the officer. Alex tried to speak but the wee nurse put her hand over his mouth and whispered, "Try not to speak. Save your energy. You've been through a lot and need to mend a spell." Alex had wanted to know what the captain meant when he said, strong enough to reason with. The nurse dipped a sponge into a bowl of white milky liquid and dampened Alexs' lips. In a few moments Alex became drowsy and fell back to sleep. For the next few days the boy drifted in an out of dreams. During the short periods of time Alex was awake he noticed that the wee people seemed to be getting bigger. As he began to get stronger, Alex would sit up and look about the strange cavern. The doctor came often and mostly asked how Alex was feeling. When Alex asked questions the only answers he would get was, "you'll know soon enough, the ins and outs of it all." The stronger Alex became the more anxious he grew.

He thought it odd that his clothes were loose. It wasn't very long until they started bringing him changes of clothing. Usually they were bright colored togas and waist straps. The day arrived when Alex would learn the truth about himself and this strange new world.

CHAPTER 5
BARGE TO ANTON

Once again the captain was summoned. During Alexs' recuperation he had seen hundreds of soldiers, coming and going on the far bank of the river that ran through the middle of the cavern. With them were wagons filled with large rocks. The wagons came back empty. He learned quickly that he would get no answers from the guards or those attending to his health. He could but hope that the answers would come. When the captain finally came he stood head to head with Alex.

By this time, Alex knew that he was shrunk to the size of the wee people, though it was a mystery as to how or why such a thing should happen. A barge had been floated near the shore where Alex had been kept for days out of memory. The doctor again pleaded with the captain to leave Alex free. The captain sternly stated. "It is my charge to take the lad before the Council of Chevrons. Until such time as they order him free, he'll be treated like a prisoner. Besides, you have enough to worry about with the survivors of Clarion. Doctor, you mind the sick and injured and I'll tend to the military matters of the King." "Be on with your duties then captain, you can't see beyond your soldiering; so it is nonsense to try and reason with the lot of ya." Snapped the doctor.

"Aye," said the captain, "take the prisoner aboard and begin the voyage to the Council of Chevrons. Tis yet three days journey, so mind ye the supplies. Two troops will accompany, one onboard the other by land. They'll take turns at duty. Those on land beware of the lands beyond the Twin Sisters Falls. The Trogglites and Coretians are on the move."

"We'll make camp at the white waters under the falls. I want to hear drums until the sounding of my bugle to halt. No torches or pipe-smoke until break is called. Move out and stay quick." Finished the Captain.

Alex was made to sit on the deck of the barge. It was hard and cold. The doctor gave a flask of the milky white liquid to the captain with instructions for administering it to Alex. The drink made Alex drowsy and often put him to sleep with dreams. The dreams he would have were still of far away places and adventures. It made it hard for Alex to know whether he was awake or dreaming. As he heard the order to move out he heard the drum thump. It beat out three singles and a double. Over and over they beat until Alex became so used to the sound he could think without hearing them. Where am I? What is going to happen to me? How did I get here and what lay ahead? Alexs' thoughts often turned from his troubles, to his family. Where are they and are they safe? Do they know where I am and will I ever see them again? This wasn't the last time he would ask himself these questions. Alex could hear the soldiers talking. Such strange conversation pondered the lad. Talk of monstrous things. Names he had never heard of before. Often a song would be sung, telling tales of heroes, maidens, and of wars and kings. Much of what he heard sounded both, glamorous and ugly, happy and at the same time sad. He wished he could see and understand more of what was going on around him. At times, he was glad he didn't know. He was already frightened and confused enough as it was.

He was fast asleep when the shrill blast from the bugle woke him. The sounds of splashing water mixed with sighs of exhaustion from the soldiers told Alex they were taking a break. The drums had stopped and the troops were changing post. Alex could smell pipe smoke and hear laughter. He felt a wafer at his lips and the smell of honey and lemon filled his nose as he opened his mouth to eat. It tasted sweet and gave a hot flash of energy to Alex. The dream potion followed the treat, as Alex began to think of it. Soon he was fast asleep and didn't hear the barge pull off and the drums begin.

Not knowing how long he had been asleep or any sense of time at all, Alex awoke. He felt groggy and at first forgot the dilemma he was in. He slowly came around to his senses. The first sense of sound told him there was no sound except a constant roar of rushing water. He had never heard or seen a waterfall but Grandfather McNaire had told him of such things in the Blue Mountains far from the farms and flatland of Ireland. He compared what he heard with that of his grandfathers' tales and decided it must be a very, very large waterfall, indeed. There were no drums, no laughter, and not a sound of anyone talking. He wondered if he'd been left alone and what could he do all tied up.

Alex found himself being picked up and carried off the barge. Someone whispered in his ear. "You'll be fine lad, don't struggle and be very, very quiet." The two soldiers carrying Alex placed him on the ground between two boulders and placed a comforter around his shoulders.

He could hear the captain talking very low. He sent two scouting parties out on a short range patrol and bid the rest of the troop to bed down and to post watch among them-selves. He could hear zippers and snaps all around him and thought the soldiers were setting up camp. After some short whispers all he could hear was the roar of the falls. He didn't fall asleep again for quite some time but let his mind run wild again. He thought to himself, am I ever going home again? What have they done to make me so small? Will I ever grow back to my normal height? Can I see Tom and Sue and baby Sherrie and tell them, grandfathers' yarns are real? Would even grandfather believe what is happening to me? I can hardly believe it my-self.

Alex was restless. He wiggled about till he was bouncing back and forth between the two cold boulders. His feet hit something softer than rock and brought attention to a sleeping soldier. "See here, ya odd being, get yourself back to where ya ought to be." Grumbled the soldier. Alex felt a tug on his shoulders and used his heels to push himself back among the rocks. The disturbed trooper mumbled his way back into his sleeping bag and fainted out to sleep.

The next time Alex was stirred around was when he heard the commotion of the scouts returning. They were telling the captain what they had seen throughout the night. " Captain, we observed two mounted battalions of Troggs closing in toward the Southern Frontier. Escorted by a half dozen warlords. Riding slim slugs pulling three battering rams and two catapults. We lost sight of them when they marched into an enlarged mole tunnel to set up camp. The stench of them still burns my nostrils." Reported the scout. After his report the scout was dismissed to make room for the second scouts' report. "Sir, about the third hour we could see afar off to the East at least one legion, it's hard to say for sure if there were more. By the look of the torches we counted at least that many by guess. They too. Escorted by mounted Troggs. Pulling several war wagons. We did not wait for them to swarm to camp, because of the size of them. They were slowly advancing toward the outskirts of Gatalla. Perhaps four, maybe five days march from the city." Finished the second scout.

"Though your reports hold grief. Your performance is well received." Commented the Captain. "Both patrols are to eat and catch some sleep on the barge. We must proceed fast to the council chambers to deliver the prisoner and inform the Royal Prince Leroy of our findings." Stated the Captain. The barge floated for what seemed like hours to Alex. There was very little talk aboard the barge and even less laughter. There was talk of the six chevrons. What was to become of Alex was of little importance to the soldiers. War and Trogg were the main topics of conversation when there was any. The drums pounded out cadence until the bugle sounded halt.

"Troops eat quickly and smoke if you must. We will pull out in ten minutes." Shouted the Captain. There was a strong sense of concern in his voice, and Alex could hear him pace around the wooden deck. Alex caught the smell of lemon and knew it was time for him to eat. After he had eaten four wafers, he drank some of the milky fluid. He was beginning to get used to the taste of it. Just as he finished eating he heard the splash of the dredge poles entering the water. The drums started. The captain leaned over the lad and spoke to him. "You chose a bad time to drop into my world. You're the first giant I've laid eyes on. Even in your present state you look odd indeed. You don't know how fortunate you were that my troops found you first. If the evil trogglites or Troggs bother Corets' slimy troops found you, you'd probably already be dead." As the captain stomped off, Alex shivered at the thought of the captains' words. He wished to go home. Alex fought against the potion he drank until it over took him and sleep won. When next Alex awoke he heard the voice of one of the opal strapped soldiers. He was assigning guard duties and dispatched two more scouting patrols. Silence fell around Alex. Not a sound did he hear except the river rushing over stones in its midst. He closed his mind and slept till dawn.

Having returned, the scouts were briefing the captain. A loud yell woke the rest of the soldiers. It was the captain yelling, not from fright but in celebration. The news was good and refreshing. "The menacing dark enemy was nowhere in sight, reported the scouts. "Good news indeed, they've not advanced this far. In a matter of hours we'll be at the threshold of Anton. Ready the troops and fetch the lad aboard the barge. Make hast, there will be time enough to rest and feast upon our arrival at the Kings' palace." Yelled the Captain. Alex welcomed the sound of the drums as the march began. Many voices broke into song. As they sang, Alex heard distant echoes as if they were in some tremendous cavern. The song was in cadence with the beating drums. As Alex later learned those troops escorting him had been in the field for a very long time and could hardly wait to get home to their families and loved ones.

Alex was lifted to his feet as the barge docked. He heard a large number shouting and calling names from the dock. Alex was placed between two guards to his right and two more on his left. He heard their feet hit the wooden sidewalks leading away from the river. Several turns and countless greetings passed before they entered a large passage way. He was lead by the arms to a huge pair of wooden doors. As the doors were swung opened, trumpets sounded. When his small party halted so did the trumpets. A stern voice ordered the blindfold removed.

CHAPTER 6
BEFORE THE COUNCIL OF CHEVRONS

Alex was free to see, though he believed the potion was causing him to see things that could not be real. He rubbed his eyes, and then rubbed them again. Yet the sight remained unchanged. He was in a large hall and in the middle there was a horseshoe shaped table. The walls where draped with three Chevrons on the left and three to the right. At the end of the hall was a staircase leading to a large throne. The arms of the throne were made of gold fashioned in the likeness of large serpents. The eyes of the snakes were mounted rubies. Their bodies ran the length of the armrest and the tails joined up around the thrones back.

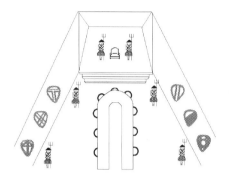

The great wooden doors were closing. He turned back to the table and took stock of its' appearance. To the left turn of the horseshoe sat three noble looking males. To the right sat three more, each was dressed in the colors and details of the Chevrons behind them on the walls. A door off to the side of the great throne opened and a figure appeared in a coarse brown tunic, with a rope wrapped around his waist shouting. "Rise, ye members of council at the presence of Prince Leroy, keeper of the kings forces, protector and provider of the throne." The six council members stood and kicked back their seats as they rose. Then entered the Prince. He was taller than most of whom Alex had seen which wasn't many. His skin was fair and his orange red hair, lay on his shoulders and his chest long beard lay in waves beneath his chin. As the prince took his seat at the crown of the horseshoe table the other six were seated.

The prince gestured to Alex to approach the inner portion of the table. He followed the jester and came to rest before the head of the table. The Princes' voice, low but frank, ordered the captain of the guard to be brought before the host. One of the council cleared his throat then spoke. "This funny looking creature is wearing a toga in the color and fashion of my peasants." "Hold your tongue, Lord of Cortane, and we will get to the heart of things." Assured the Prince. As soon as the captain arrived the pipes were lit and the council settled back for a line of questioning.

"Most honorable lords of my fathers kingdom, let the Captain speak. If his testimony leaves you with unanswered questions, we'll deal with them at that time." Said the Prince.

Alex was most attentive as the captain gave his account, of how he had come to be in the spot he was in. "Sir." began the captain, "three days ago a storm blew across the outer world in the lands of the giants. Even as the storm blew, the people of Clarion went on with their simple business. Without warning, an ear splitting crack was heard and in seconds the great tree of Clarion was divided to its' roots. The ground above began to topple and cover Clarion. Then, from the midst of this tragic event, fell the lad. Not of his own choice, I'm sure, but just the same his monstrous body crushed parts of the village. Between him and the earth, Clarion was all but demolished."

"The water that ran next to the great tree over flowed and with out the roots of the tree to trap the water, it poured down on the village. Those who weren't crushed were flooded from their homes." "We have now taken the sick and injured to a make shift hospital." "As my troops removed the peasants, a tremendous task is under way to cover any signs of our kingdom." "The farming giants will cut up the tree for fire wood and probably fill the hole the great tree has left." "Excellent work on your part captain, and you may be sure your reward for loyalty to the kingdom will be as excellent. You may take leave to continue your duties after your troops have cleaned and refreshed themselves. Thank you," finished Prince Leroy.

"Council, I have here before me tablets of the doctor who made possible this boys' presence." "The lad was struck on the head as the great tree was split." "He didn't wake for several days." "The doctor took it upon himself to administer Quantine." "Council, you are all more familiar than I with the effects of this medicine." "Aye," acknowledged the council members. "In my young age I but vaguely heard of it's use on the larger Dwarfs." "Never have I thought it would be used again." "The doctors' reasoning seems logical." "Had the lad awakened in his normal size, panic could of caused much worse damage than was already done." "I choose not to bring charges against the doctor for his courage and best interest of us all." "Agreed." Said the council." "Now lad it's an awkward situation you've placed us in."

"Tell us your story." Finished the Prince. "I really haven't a story, sir." Said Alex. "Did you ever dream that my people were real, not just myth and legend?" "Of course some of the tales I've over heard are a bit far fetched." Asked one of the council members. "Yes sir, they are, but yes I knew you were real." "Well not you exactly, but some Leprechauns I knew were real." Remarked Alex "How is that?" Asked the Prince. "I've seen one." Stated Alex. "You have?" Questioned the Lord of the hall. "That cannot be. It is forbidden in these times for a leprechaun to show himself in the outer world." Snapped the Prince. "I didn't say he showed himself to me," replied Alex. "It was his misfortune that I even saw him." "What was his appearance, lad?" Came a question from a councilman. "Sir, I have no desire to get one of your people into mischief." Commented Alex. "Mischief. Is not the lot of it, lad, such a sacred thing will not go unpunished." Replied the questioning councilman.   Alex looked around the table. All the faces were cold and scornful.

"I've urgent military council with my generals." "I cannot be tied up with this matter very long." "If you don't wish to tell me the violator at least I address the honorable soul of you." "You probably have a thousand questions and deserve answers to most of them." "For the time being, I leave you to the charge of the council." "Whatever they declare, I will honor." "Only thing I ask is that the lad not be harmed in any way until I have heard all the arguments of the council." "At present, I want this matter kept from my father, the king." "He has enough on his mind with Trogg and Coret with their armies moving again after decades of peace." "Lords of the Chevrons, I leave you to suit my armor and sharpen my arrows." "I journey to each of your lands, and take council with your armies." "They must answer my call and know my plans." "Keep the lad within sight." "Teach him only of what he needs to know." "'Tis a chance he may never leave." Ended Prince Leroy. They stood from the table with a snap as the prince stood, clasp his fist to his chest in salute, with his ring hand upon the covered hilt of his sword. The cap of the hilt was made the same as the throne, the head of a serpent with ruby eyes.

After the prince had left, one of the councilmen spoke. "What is your name, lad?" "I am Alex, sir." "Good. Alex, I am Satchen, Council of Sir Kenneth, Knight of the king, to the City of Gattala." "You will wait in the outer chamber until we decide what is to be done with you." Stated Satchen. Alex was then escorted out of the great hall. Moments later Satchen came out from the wooden doors. "Follow me, lad." Directed Satchen. The two began a long walk down the corridor. On both sides were statues and busts. "These, lad are fore fathers of leprechauns." "On the morrow I will begin to tutor you in the lore of my people." "At times you are not in study, you will be left to be with me nephew." Said Satchen.

CHAPTER 7
ALEX MEETS LEAPPY

Alex took in as much as his big eyes would allow. Satchen and Alex passed through a stone arch, down a long stairway, into the courtyard. The lad gasped! "Oh, St. Christopher, where have you brought me?" There was light in the courtyard, light similar to that of day. "How can it be?" Ask Alex. "Mind yourself lad, your questions will be answered." Answered Stachen. He saw many colors, soft purple with floating pink and blues mixing in. In the center of the courtyard was a fountain with big, brightly painted Monarch butterflies weaving in and out of the jets of water. The high dome ceiling was polished and looked like marble. The fountain flowed down a slue to the river. Children were playing in the blue grass of a park next to the river and the sounds of a calliope could be heard in a jolly tune. Alex noticed women and children and old men. There were lads his age, no young men. The war he thought. From the casual stroll, the pair went through a picket fence into a small yard, into a small house. At least it looked small from the outside. When Alex entered the threshold it shook him to see the inside of a mansion. He wanted to go back out and come in again but Satchen gently took his shoulder and turned him back around.

"Come now Alex, enough for one day don't you think?" Asked the councilman. "No, I mean yes, I guess so sir," stammered Alex. "You're a well-mannered lad, Alex." "Perhaps you'll be as much of an influence on me nephew as he will be in teaching you the what's and whys of it all." Satchen motioned Alex to follow him into a sitting room. He pulled on a silver threaded rope and chimes sounded. A woman appeared and was given instructions to bring drink and wafers. Then, she was told to find his nephew and send him in. Satchen sat at a highly polished, wooden desk, opened a tobacco canister and took a pinch to put in the bowl of a stem pipe. Then took another and still a third, packed in down with a pipe nail. When he had lit the pipe he leaned back and stared at the ceiling a moment then blew smoke rings. This told Alex the councilman was not always all business. The quiet was short lived as the door slammed shut and a shrill voice shouted, "Uncle, Uncle, what's this tale of a giant turned;" he cut his question short when he saw Alex sitting on the divan. "Alex, this is Lepriono." "We call him Leappy." Introduced Satchen. When the two lads laid eyes on one another they knew it wasn't the first time they had met.

"The politics of the matter is none of your concern. Never before has such things taken place. Until it's determined what should be done in the matter, you're to keep the lad company." Ordered Satchen. "But uncle, he looks so odd, me friends will laugh at me." "Never the less, Leappy, you will keep him company even if it means staying in the mansion. Now take Alex with you and show him your rooms and get him settled." Instructed Satchen.

"You both may have a snack first." Added Satchen. "So it tis," frowned Leappy. Alex was wondering why this leprechaun lad had whiskers and looked to be fifty if a day. I'll ask him when we're alone, thought Alex.

After refreshment the boys were excused to their

quarters. "It will take some getting used to, having you around." Said Leappy. " Yes and the same for me." Said Alex. Well, I want to thank you for not spilling the beans on me about the tarts and all," said Leappy. You're welcome. Said Alex. Thank you for returning my handkerchief." "Pretty good trick, wasn't it?" "I'll have you know that you're a rodent now, too." Said Leappy. The both of them broke out in laughter.

"Leappy why do you have a beard?" Ask Alex. Leappy played back, "why do you not have one?" "I'm just fifteen years old." Stated Alex. "Yes I see, well in my realm at 15 we have hair on our chins." Replied Leappy. "Yuk," jested Alex. "Yuk, yourself," said Leappy, "Here you're the one that is out of place. Since you didn't squeal on me I guess we can work something out. I could have been in deep hot water if the elders knew I was on the surface, let alone being seen." "There are whole clans of leprechauns whose purpose in life is to keep up with the world outside. They are raised in the art of not getting caught. We here below must know such things as the weather, and the where abouts of the giants and their work." "Leappy, there have been many times people have reported seeing leprechauns," said Alex. "Aye, but could they prove it?

Did they catch any?" Questioned Leappy. "Well no," said Alex. "Get me point?" Said Leappy. "What did you mean when you said, work something out?" Asked Alex. "Ya can't go running around with me, looking bare faced as a pixie." Answered Leappy. It didn't set well with Alex to be compared like that. "What can we do about it?" Asked Alex. "Well, we are not staying in. Wait here in the room and I'll be right back," said Leappy.

Right back he was, with a pair of shears and some glue. "Wait, just wait a minute. What do you intend to do with those?" Asked Alex. "Come now Alex, you've got to work with me on this, or I'll be boxed up here." Pleaded Leappy. "After dinner me uncle takes a pipe in the garden out back, then retires early for the night." "I have some friends for you to meet." "Come now Alex." "Would you rather sit here and worry of matters you have no way of changing?" "We will just trim enough of the hair off the top of your head, to make you a face piece." "Won't your friends still know I'm not a," "a what, Alex?" Interrupted Leappy. "A leprechaun where ya about to say?" "Well, I'll have you know lad, some of me best friends are leprechauns." Jested Leappy. The two of them began to laugh so hard tears came to their eyes.

The chimes sounded for dinner and the two lads ran down the hall and slid down the banister. They cleared their throats and wiped the smiles off their faces as they entered the dining room. Satchen was already seated when they pulled their chairs up to the table. Alex could smell something wonderful but, of course, he had no idea what it was. He passed his dish to Satchen and watched him ladle from a silver bowl a thick, chunky stew. It smelled delicious and he found the taste just as rewarding. After second helpings of stew, the lads were excused. "Alex." Called Satchen, "mind you don't wander off from here alone. You're on your word of honor. Don't make me have to look for you. If it is that way, you won't like your new quarters." Said Satchen. "What does he mean Leappy, new quarters?" Asked Alex. "The dungeon," whispered Leappy. "Hurry now, let's get you ready." Satchen walked through his garden with his hand folded behind his back. The boys watched him stroll and thought he'd never come in. "Leappy are we breaking any rules by going out?" "No Alex, we're not." "It's just that I don't want my uncle to see you before we leave." "Oh," said" Alex, "I see." Alex and Leappy made a quick job of the beard. When Alex looked in the mirror he was tickled and found it rather handsome.

They made their way out into the courtyard. The whole city was engulfed in a pale blue light and the fountain gave off sparkles of tiny flakes of silver; like diamonds. Alex was so full of discovering new sights and sounds he all but forgot his misfortune. They made their way to the river. The sides of the immense cavern were dotted with torches that put off enough light to guide a boat across the river of crystal clear waters. "Alex, see that group of lights over there?" Ask Leappy. Alex followed Leappys' pointing finger and saw what he was referring to. "Yes, I do," said Alex. "That's where we'll meet my friends." "When we moor the gondola let me do the talking first." "At least your face won't spook them none." Said Leappy. "Thanks a lot, friend," said Alex. "You're very welcome, leprechaun," ventured Leappy. They were quietly approaching an island from which they heard laughter and voices. The sleek gondola moored silently ashore. Alex and Leappy were almost on top of the bon-fire before they were noticed.

"Leappy, you startled us," came a girls voice from the shadows. "I'll have you know I've had me beauty sleep, and there is no way I could be so ugly as to scare a lot such as you." Replied Leappy. "Come sit with me Leappy," said the voice softly and with purpose. "Yes, in a moment Dona my love." "First I want everyone to meet my cousin, Alex." Said Leappy. "I didn't know you had a cousin," said a sharp, rude voice. "Well, I do Brock, so be civil to him." "His father, my uncle, was jumped and murdered by trogglites and his mother carried off." Stated Leappy. "How awful, said another female voice." "We are all glad to make your acquaintance." "Aren't we tribe?" Finished the voice. Alex heard. "Yes, of course," as faces came toward the light of the fire. "Alex, come with me to the boat and help with the keg of ale from uncles cellar." Implied Leappy. As they walked to the boat, Leappy said, "I know there is a lot of questions you need answers to. Take my advice, keep your eyes and ears open and your mouth closed. You will learn a lot more a lot quicker." "I agree," said Alex. "One more thing; stay away from Brock." said Leappy.

CHAPTER 8
AROUND THE BON-FIRE

As Alex and Leappy rolled the keg of ale toward the bon fire the laughter hit a memory in Alex and he was instantly sad. As in his minds eye he remembered the laughter and sounds of founders-day back home. Leappy said, "Alex, maybe this isn't such a good idea." "Alex please, I know times are hard on you, everything will work out for the best no matter how it happens, it will." "Remember, eyes and ears open" began Leappy, "yes, yes," interrupted Alex "and mouth shut." "I'll try, but I want you to know my heart isn't in it." As Alex finished saying that, the lads came into the glow of the bon-fire. "Leappy, you're a true trooper," smarted Brock. "Let me help you up with that." Leappy and Brock sat the keg on end as Dona handed them the tap and mallet. The ale was shaken and a splash of foam shot up and splattered Brock in the face. Howls of laughter broke out as he wiped his face and licked his fingers. "Still, I tapped it with just one blow," said Brock. "Oh, Brock my hero," giggled one of the girls. "It's best to let it settle a bit before you open the tap," Leappy told them. "Meanwhile how about some introductions."

"Sure, all right I'll start." Said Dona. "Welcome Alex my name is Dona my father is Sir Duram, knight of the King in the city of Cortain. Next to me is my best female friend, Jessica. "Hi again Alex my name as Dona said is Jessica my eldest brother is Sir Ivan, knight of the king in the city of Cornalla. Across from you by the keg is Brock." "I hope my bad manners didn't scare you none," said Brock. "My father is Sir Phillip of Philane, knight to the king, and here to my right is squash head." "I'm sorry, I mean Gordon." "Real funny, Brock Lee," said Gordon." "I'm Gordon from Clarion, my father was Sir Aldain, knight of the king." "I m very sorry, they haven't yet found my father since the great tree above our city split and started and avalanche of mud and stone and a tremendous flood washed out my home." "Come," said Jessica, "let me hold your hand, Gordon. We are all with you and there is still a very big possibility your father is still alive." As Jessica consoled Gordon a voice that sounded almost mechanical spoke out. "My name is Yota, son of Yerta, knight of the king in Urbane, ruler of the North." As he stood, Yota was tall and slender like Prince Leroy with much the same features. Yota was darker skinned and his hair golden blond, beard, head, arms, and legs. He was dressed in the garb of a soldier. His shoulder straps were studded with emeralds and a garnet the size of a walnut in the center where the straps crossed. Around his waist he wore a sword on one hip and a dagger on the other. Around his neck and across his back hung a quiver of arrows and beside him lay a bow. It was as long as Yota was tall.

Leappy stood and took Alex by the hand and led him in front of a girl with her head bowed. She sat just to the edge of the shadows and her auburn red hair dropped across her narrow shoulders. "Alex, the best come last." "It's forbidden by tradition for her to address any male, until they are properly introduced."

"Lady Dora. Is Princess and daughter of King Anton, from the city with his name." Said Leappy. As the girl lifted her head and opened her eyes to look at Alex his heart beat began to race. He gazed into the depth of her green eyes and was completely taken with her beauty. Never before had Alex felt such an experience. She turned her head to one side and said, "Hello, Alex, I am pleased to meet you." "I'm sure," mumbled Alex, "that is, I'm sure I am glad you're pleased." "Alex don't stutter now, and don't feel awkward. The Lady Dora can have that effect on one," said Leappy. Leappy guided Alex back across the circle and sat him on a rock, cushioned with a quilt. Alex couldn't seem to take his eyes off the princess. Leappy slapped his hands together in front of Alexs' face to break the trance. "Ale, any one?" Asked Brock. All but Yota said yes. He only stood, took a piece of root from a pouch on his wrist and bit off a chunk and chewed it. As they continued to joke with one another, Alex was trying not to stare across the flames but could hardly help himself. "How about a story? One that can help Alex understand why so many heads of states' kindred are here in Anton, said Gordon." "Good idea," said the rest. "What kind of a story?" Asked Brock. "I know, let's tell the Tale of the Seven Crystals," said Gordon. "It's long, the night is young, and the keg is full. We can take turns. If one of us gets stuck the rest can help fill in the missing parts." It didn't take much convincing on Leappys' part. He seemed to be a natural leader. "I'll start," said Leappy. The company became ghostly quiet. Leappy licked his lips and began.

"In the past, long before antiquity lived the elfin Monarchs. They ruled a fair race of a happy sort. The elfin Lords ruled the sky, mountains, forest, and abundant plains of flowers and streams. Long before the Dwarf walked among them were their numbers and powers great. Such beauty has never since been seen. The song of the wood nymph was soft as a mid-summers breeze and as light as a rose petal. The elves were master with their hands. They took gold and silver and forged and beat them into find threads, which they sewed into gifts for the Queen, who lived on the crown of a great mountain. Looking over the world beneath her feet. Her beauty was too much for mortal giants to look upon. Her song started the elves singing and merry making. On her head she wore a crown with seven crystals. There were three to the left, three to the right and the largest on top in the center. When the sun shown upon the face of the Queen, the crystals split the light into colors that jetted from her throne to every corner of her kingdom.

The elves were skilled in the arts, music of harp, and horn. They used their hands to build beautiful cities. Not before dwarf and giant did their hands need to forge weapons. They were a peaceful people. They were never angry, never ill, and never an enemy of any.

The magic of the elves was in their song. The spirit of Queen Aurelie was with and in all the children of merriment. It's not known how long the queen watched the evil of dwarfs move ever nearer her vast domain. Not that dwarfs were evil. For at first elves only knowing, good, truth, love, and simplicity opened the gates of their kingdom. It is said that the magic and powers of the queen could cure and heal.

The dwarfs in the beginning of that time lived and learned much from Auriles children. They lived in harmony for time uncounted. The dwarfs though not as nimble as the elf, were talented miners of gold, silver, and precious stones. At that time the dwarfs labor was bent on mining. The elves would have no part of being hidden in a dark clammy hole, out of the sight of their beloved queen. The elves loved the smell of nature and the freshness of life and in being active. The dwarfs traded food and drink for raw materials to further their art. The dwarf out side of their rough talents did have a draw back, greed. They were fair in trade, but gave nothing without something in return. Like I've said, repeated Leappy, on their own merit dwarfs are not bad. Not refined and good mannered perhaps, but not violent. Aurelie while singing her morning serenade, for her children, saw the reason for the dwarfs' flight into her lands. It froze her heart with grief to see the human approach her valleys. As they came painfully slow, they cut and burned and lay to waste the fibers of her court. Trees were cut, fields burned, and the friends and playmates of her race, the animals, were killed and lay to rot. As the menace moved closer the Queen called for the King of the dwarfs and her strongest and quickest wood elf. They formed a league. The dwarfs King, Zarn was instructed to teach the elves war and weapons.

CHAPTER 9
UNDER GROUND

The day came when the giants were close and the Queen took off her crown of seven crystals. She had sent patrols to observe the humans approach. She summoned King Zarn. "Zarn, I leave in your charge my most wise and trained in your art of war. They are the elders of my elves. They will fight till their death. To allow my children of the meadows and streams to sail with me across the skies, for this one purpose do they stand with you. We must flee to the kingdom of my fore fathers. The elves of the woods will remain. I leave you to their fate. Teach them well how to make a life under the earth. Here they will remain until my return. My eldest and most beloved son, Yentle, will carry my crown before my people to remind them of my love and devotion." Said the Queen.

The Queen called all her beloved elfin tribes together. King Zarn formed his legions. The Queens broken heart, went with them all. She commanded great white clouds to settle at the feet of her throne. The elves climbed on with their harps, flutes and unshaken love of their lady Aurelie. The wind came up and bore them out of sight but never even until this day, out of memory.

Zarn and Yentle met mankind head on at the edge of the Queens domain. Arrows flew and the battle-ax of the dwarf swung. The battle raged heavy for four days and on the eve of the fourth day, Zarn, lay in the arms of Yentle, dieing. "Yentle my dwarfs fight because we have been pursued longer than I can trace my bloodline back to the most ancient of dwarfs." "The elf has been kind to us and shown us much we had forgotten. Call to me my brothers son Zul." "I will leave my final charges with him." "It is time gentle elf to take your brethren and retreat to the mines under Aurelies' gardens." "My kin will remain with me to cover your flight." "If any of my kin survive they will join you, If not you must lead your kind into their destiny." "The crown of your Lady will provide all your needs." "Always keep watch on man least he find you." "The secrets of elves, lives with you." "Rule wisely Yentle." "Now leave in haste I must speak with Zul."

Yentle returned with those dwarfs whom were not slain, together with the woodelves. The dwarfs managed to halt the advance of the giants long enough for the elves to gather in what now is Anton. The children of Aurelie and the dwarfs of Zarn began a new kingdom below the earth. As the older ones lived together at work for a common good they married and brought forth children. These children had some of the magic of Aurelie and much of the skills of Zarn. As the new kingdom grew, certain lords would start colonies and develop cultures of their own. Yentle was forefather many generations ago to the race Yota belongs to. Zarns' great, great, great, etc. grandchildren, is best represented by Brocks' clan. With the wisdom of Yentle and the skills of the dwarf, the crown of Aurelie was dismantled. The large center crystal is atop the tower of Anton. Constructed by Zarns kin. In the midst of a canyon directly over the crystal is the orifice of Zarn, believed to be the tomb of the great king.

As the sun rises, the crystal splits the suns rays. This supplies the kingdom with light. The colors each represent a part of our queen. As the clans migrated so went with each a crystal. Each placed on its' own tower in each of the six cities. The light of Anon reflects to each of the cities and provides the needs of sunlight to our people. So it has been to this day. Each clan provides one member of its' royal family as envoy to Anton. This is mostly from tradition. To insure the clans survival in the event of a mishap such as has taken place in Clarion. Also the Council of Chevrons was formed to make law and keep the peace." "Well," said Leappy "that's about the long and short of it." "Good" said Gordon. "That made me thirsty." Those around the bon-fire began to talk and laugh among themselves. Yota, was still standing alone and was approached by Alex. "That was a great yarn." Began Alex. "Sure," grunted Yota. "Can you tell me about the Troggs and why we tried to avoid them on the way from Clarion to Anton?" Ask Alex "Yes," is all Yota would reply. Alex thought Yes, but what? Yes I could tell you, or Yes, I could tell you but I won't, or just plain yes, if you ask me again. So Alex went with his last thought and asked Yota again. "Would you let our friends finish their refreshment and enjoy the night?" "I will tell you of Trogg and other ugly matters at a less exiting time." "Go now and join Leappy and the others and forget such serious matters until latter." "It is not for me to say in front of the others, but you are a stranger to my world." "I know and my clan knows the things taking place in this kingdom." "Leappy is young and foolish at times but a true friend if ever there was one." "It is for this I hold my tongue." "I trust his judgment and know in time he will tell us what he feels need be told." "Enjoy yourself and may all go well with you." Finished Yota.

Alex was surprised, not as being recognized as an outsider, but at Yotas' belief in a friend, such as to hold his tongue. He held wisdom beyond his years. Gordon, Brock, and Yota left the gathering only to return with instruments from their gondolas. Yota sat a slender silver harp under an awning of tree branches. He then returned to where he had been standing the whole time of the story telling. With Yota was a flute of ebony-black adorned with carvings and markings. Markings Alex could not read nor had he ever seen them before. Brock carried a horn of some animal on a velvet sling. Brock handed a mandolin to Leappy. Dona sat herself with the harp while Jessica reached to her side for a golden piccolo. The Princess Dora sat but calm and serene. Alex not taken to drinking ale sat back on his stone chair and relaxed.

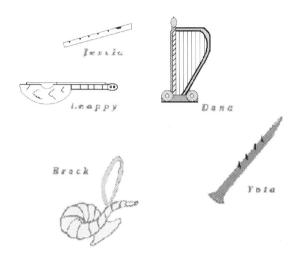

The strings of the harp began in a slow soft almost mystical sound. The others joined and began to blend with Dona. Alex closed his eyes and let his mind drift. He felt lightheaded and almost feel to sleep when he heard Doras' voice begin to melt and flow with the music when she started into song. Words Alex never heard. They were the language of the elf. Alexs' thoughts turned to the Tale of the Seven Crystals. They painted meadows of yellow, red, violet, and blue flowers in soft green grass. A bubbly stream ran into a forest of spruce and fur with glints of sunlight piercing the shade of them.

The song was warm and soothing. Doras' voice seemed as a breeze that softly swayed the grass in the fields of Alexs' dream.

The night slipped away. Alex not knowing when he had fallen asleep was awaken by his new companion Leappy. "It is time to return Alex before my uncle awakens." "Come now, the others have already gone." Stated Leappy. As he rubbed the sleep from his eyes Alex could see the enormous cavern was filled with a pinkish light. The gondola glided into dock. "Leappy was I, I mean did everything go ok?" Asked Alex. "Yes Alex you were fine and well received. Yota spoke with me about your inquiry of Trogg. Yota will let you know when it is time. He is the most versed in the lore of Trogg and Coret. For now Alex you need finish your sleep. I will wake you when Uncle Satchen calls for you. It will be late in the day for he is in council until mid-day meal." Said Leappy.

"Afterwards he can tell you of his purpose and what the council of Chevrons had discussed." "Their wisdom is greater than that of man, they will be fare and just." "You have heard much in a short time, think on that but don't try to understand it all." "You've left a good impression on my friends." "We all wish only for the good of our kind and what is right for you." "Rest now and I will call you later." Finished Leappy. Alex without much effort undressed and drifted back to the quite of the fields in his dreams and was soon at sleep.

Alex slept the morning hours away. Leappy woke him with the strong smell of tea. "Here I've brought you something to eat and drink." Smiled Leappy. On the tray with his breakfast was a small glass cup with the white milky liquid. Leappy poured it into the dark brewed tea and handed it to Alex. "After you've eaten. I've left some garments on the stool by the door. My Uncle had his tailor make them for you. Though my friends and the council know who and what you are, you must, at least for now, stay a secret to the rest of the city." Said Leappy as he left.

Alex finished eating, washed up and began to dress in his new cloths. Strange indeed thought Alex, the fit is perfect. He began to admire himself in the looking glass of the bureau. A white frilled shirt with stone buttons. There was a pair of knickers of dark green. It was a deeper green than leappys'. With a matching vest, high socks, highly glossed shoes with a side strap snap. To top it all off was a matching green hat with a silver buckle. "If Thomas could see me now," smiled Alex to himself in front of the mirror. This thought brought sadness to Alex and a tear formed in Alexs' eye. If only I could see Thomas now, puckered Alex. The door to his snuggery opened and Leappy told him they must make haste. "Uncle has called for you now Alex, come, come." Out of the house, through the gate and down the path went the pair. "I must meet with Yota and Brock, but I will see you this-evenings meal." "In respect I must still caution you not to ask too many questions. My Uncle will tell you what the council wants you to know." "For your own freedom, I warn you not to upset Uncle Satchen." "It's not to the elders pleasure that you are here at all." Commented Leappy. They arrived in front of the tower of Anton. Over the arched door flew seven flags. Each flag was a different color. Each flag bore a chevron coat of arms. After Leappy showed Alex into the long hall of armor and sculptures, he bid a good day to Alex and departed for his meeting. Shortly thereafter the great wooden doors slowly opened and Satchen came through them.

CHAPTER 10
TROGG AND CORET

"Well now lad, I trust you've been entertained by my nephew?" Asked Satchen. "Yes Sir," said Alex.

"Hum, I'll bet indeed you have. Well come with me now lad let us talk." Satchen replied. Alex and Satchen left the hall and strolled along the banks of the river until they came to a park with fountains and sat on an iron bench. Satchen packed his pipe. Alex noticed in the light of day Satchen was old, very old and the look of him demanded respect. The elders' eyes were clear and sharp, filled with knowledge and deep thought.

"Young man," Satchens voice was stern with heavy emphases on the man. "You've put council in a circumstance new to all of us." "This circumstance has come at a bad time." "Matters that should not involve you or giants at all have now come to the point, we feel you should know the grave dangers you are in." "Not by your choice, we're aware of that." "It was also not a matter of your choice to be here at all, but here you are." "We have not seen the Lord of Clarion since the terrible storm that destroyed the city." "Almost all the citizens are accounted for." Satchens' voice broke as the last word reluctantly came out. "Only the doctor, nurse, and Captain that was assigned to Clarion, know you are human." "It was by the doctors reasoning you've, become the size you are now." "He began giving you the Milk of Quantine. An ancient flower that grows only in the shadows of the Twin Sisters Falls."

"The supply of this potion is little." "It was discovered and used for the dwarfs in the first days of our kingdom." Alex looked startled. "It's alright, it was by my instruction that you were at the court of Royal Children." "Leappy and the others were told about you and given charge to keep you at ease until your future can be decided." "I see he did his job well by the looks of your whiskers." "His idea I venture." Mused Satchen. "Yota Sir, did he know?" "Yes said Satchen, but Yota is an Elwarf, more elf than dwarf." "His people are full of mystery and still wait for their Queens return." "He is of the blood-line of Yeta whose forefather was Yentle an Elfin Lord." Alex wanted to tell Satchen he knew the story but remembered the advice of Leappy. "Enough history, the present is enough of an adventure for you, I warrant." Said Satchen. "You have much to learn of the troubles you are in." "Many of which are shared with the Kingdom of Anton." "Trogg the eldest of two brothers is an evil, black hearted, ruthless Lord of the dark." "Coret is equal in strength and number." "He is as horrible as Trogg." "Their only difference is age." "I tell you this much to inform you, Quantine is not a flower of beauty but of rare powers." "Troggs' kingdom is growing and his shadow over looks the Twin Sisters." "Soon he will control that whole region." "Do you see the seriousness?" "Your needs will soon consume the small supply on hand." "Scientist with Yotas' people, are working as I speak." "They seek between our science and the magic of elf medicine, to find an alternative to Quantine." "Until such time one is found you are here as a guest not a prisoner." "It is to your own good to let as few as possible, know you're a lad of humans." Stated Satchen. "Yes Sir," remarked Alex. "Trogg and Coret were cast out long ago for greed and quest for power." "They want the Crystal of Anton so as to rule our world." "If they succeed we are all doomed to perish as the way of things now." "There are other dangers, how many others depend on you." "I will explain more about these when we have more details on the progress involving your size." "The shadows are creeping towards Anton and our satellites to the South." "Until then, do you know your way back to my home from here?" Questioned Satchen. "I believe so Sir, just put me on the right path." Alex replied. "Good lad, I have another session late this after noon. Inform Leappy to proceed with evening meal without me if I am too late." Said Satchen.

Satchen walked with Alex to the path of the great hall that led to Satchens cottage. "Good day lad." Said the elder. "Good day to you Sir," bid Alex. He shuffled his feet and began his short walk. Alex in deep wonder searched the huge cavern as he walked. The light had turned from the pinkish hue of morning to a faint blue.

He began to think of his troubles, those from the council, and mostly from Satchen. He shook his head as if trying to remove the thoughts because they made him afraid. He passed the fountain and noticed butterflies playing tag with the sprays of water as they flew in and out of a rainbow made by the fountain and from the crystal on the Tower of Anton.

He reached the gate of the cottage and stood looking at the great cavern in wonder, of how big this kingdom could be. Alex closed the gate. As he reached for the door handle to the cottage, the door opened, it startled him.

Leappy a bit shaken as well had opened the door from the inside. The two of them looked at each other wide eyed and began to giggle. "Come in Alex, evening meal is set at the table." "After we eat we will meet me comrades." "There is a special treat we have planned for you." As they ate Alex told Leappy what his Uncle Satchen had said. He started asking Leappy questions about the strange flower, about magic and science. "Slow up Alex and let your food settle some." "There will be time enough for you to learn of such things, without so many questions." Said Leappy. "I'm sorry Leappy, it's just I'm a little afraid of what all has happened and fear what may come." Stated Alex. "This is not good Alex, since you don't know what lay ahead." "If you must think of tomorrow before it gets here, why not think of good things?" Leappy said.

Alex wasn't sure he could do that, but he did try. The longer he was in Anton the more he missed home and his family. The adventure was fun at times but he felt that something awful was going to happen any minute. Leappy tried to keep Alexs' mind on happier things, but he knew his new friend was sad, as he would be if he dropped into a strange world away from his friends and family.

CHAPTER 11
UNDER THE FALLS OF APHILIA

The two had finished eating and put the table things away. "Will Dora be there?" asked Alex. "Of course," said Leappy, "Dona will be there too." "Yota and the others are waiting on the island for us as we speak." "Alex, my uncle and the council of Chevrons are as anxious to return you to your home as you are to get there." "Please try to have patience." "They are working hard but have other pressing matters, as well." "Tonight we will show you that you haven't as much to fear from Trogg and Coret as you have the milk of Quantine running out before you get home." Ended Leappy.

Leappy and Alex pushed off the dock and the gondola slipped quietly across the river. The light was now almost purple and growing darker as they approached the island. There were three other gondolas moored on the shore as they slowly came in. One was much the same as Leappy's craft. A second was longer and narrower. The third was somewhat wider with a small canopy to the rear. It was white and trimmed in gold with the shield of Anton on the bough. Gordon came up to Alex and said, "Alex, you escort the Princess and Yota." "I will travel with Leappy. Alex stepped out of the boat. As he did, he saw Yota board the white craft. In one hand Yota carried a torch. Gordon lit his torch from Yota's and in turn lit a third torch, which he handed to Brock. Dona and Gordon boarded Leappy's gondola. Brock and Jessica in Brock's gondola pulled away from shore first. Next the princess craft, followed by Leappy's. Alex sat in the middle of the white boat with his back to Yota at the bough. Dora sat on a small throne like chair under the canopy, facing Alex. Alex could feel his cheeks blush, as he kept his head bowed, with his eyes looking up at the princess. "Good evening, Alex. You won't be able to see much with your head down like that. It's a short while to where we are going but your neck will surely become stiff before then." said Dora. Alex lifted his head and said, "Good evening to you, princess." "Where, by the way are we going?" "Not to spoil the fun for you, Alex, but it is a surprise." "I myself haven't been there for a very long time." Answered the Princess. The gondolas were well out of sight of the city. By the light of the torch, Alex gazed into the eyes of Dora. Shimmers of light danced from her face. "Alex, it's not polite to stare," laughed Dora. "Are you able to enjoy my kingdom?" "Yes, princess, as much as I can under the conditions," answered Alex. "Tell me of your world, Alex." "Tell me about your family." "Sure, princess," said the lad. He told her of grandfather and of stories he would tell of leprechauns, pixies and elves. The Princess seemed very amused by his telling her of his life and of his family. "Such wonderful pictures your story paints, Alex." "What is your sky like?" "Tell me, Alex." "Tell me about stars and clouds." "My father used to tell me of such things, but of late he seems too busy with problems and all." As Alex shared conversation with Dora, he began to hear a faint, rumbling sound. The sound became louder and louder. Alex turned to face forward. It was another waterfall.

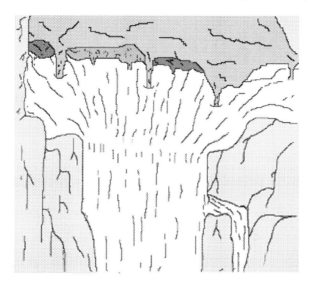

The gondolas began steering for shore toward an opening between two large boulders. They threaded their way through the twin rocks into a small stream that emptied into the river.

The stream was just wide enough for one boat at a time. The rush of the falling water drowned out any chance of conversation. Alex had never seen or imagined such a beautiful sight. The trio took a bend in the stream. After the turn, they were on the inside of the fall. Into a tunnel that opened into a large cave. The cave was illuminated by hundreds of torches. Down both sides were long rows of ships and barges. Brock pulled the first of the company's small gondolas into a dock, where two soldiers tied off the bowlines. After all three boats were tied the guards helped the Princess off and onto the wooden walk way. They bowed to Dora and snapped their fist to their swords as Yota passed. The ships had dozens of windows with oars sticking out of them. On the decks were crossbows lining each side with arrows, stacked high by each bow. At the front of each ship was a battering ram. The barges had one catapult, each with assorted size stones. Barrels of tar sat on tri-pods with stone basins to hold kindling for fire. They walked past dozens and dozens of these war ships before coming to the far end of the cave. As they approached, Alex noticed small fires spotted the darkness at the back of the cave. These were campfires for hundreds of soldiers. "Come," said Yota. "We will enter the tent of my general in charge of this fleet." Once inside, they found many pillows thrown on the floor. "These are to sit on. A guard will bring food and drink," said the general. "My Lord Yota, I will be on board my vessel." "Should you need me, you've but to call." "Thank you, general, you may retire for the night." "We are well provided for," answered Yota. The general bowed to Dora, clamped his fist to his sword, and backed out the door. "Now, Alex, do you feel any safer than before?" asked the Princess.

"Yes, I do. But safe from what?" asked Alex. "Friend, I told you once before your questions would be answered," scowled Yota. "This is but one of many fleets." "I also have many foot soldiers. We meet here tonight still as a group of friends to share in merriment." "Here, only because I await word from the south this night." "The enemy is black, dark, and death moves with him." "His shadows grow nearer, he is not to be taken lightly." "You see here but a little of our force."

"Trogg and Coret have numbers of soldiers and slug troops; their murky waters breed snakes and turtles whose jaws can sink a barge." "Alex, it is not yet time for you to hear the whole story of Trogg." "It is best told you in the light of day." "Evil lurks in the shadows and foul ears may be about." "Soon, too soon, I am afraid, the council will meet and the fate of our kingdom will be weight." "To strike first is my wish, with secrecy and speed." "No matter the decision of council, I will fight under their wisdom," finished Yota. He then searched the eyes of his friends. No one would dispute with him. Not out of fear, but from respect. "Enough of war for now." "Come, let's be merry while we wait." "It has been long since our Princess has visited the Fall of Alphillia." "Yes, Yota, it has been a long time since we came to these falls to swim in its bay." "What was once filled with our laughter is now filled with ships of sorrow," said Dora. "For this, my lady, I am sorry and wish, for your sake, that it will one day return to the place of your memories," remarked Yota.

As the company talked among themselves, a guard came in. "Forgive me, Lord Yota, for this interruption, but a messenger has been seen approaching the fall." "You are forgiven guard, bring the runner here to me when he arrives." Requested Yota. "As you say, Lord Yota," replied the guard. A silence fell over them all. "Friends, I must say, I am sorry the merry making has been short," said Yota. "We understand." "We are with you Yota, our future is in your keep." answered Dora. "You may remain here and I will receive the runners' news aboard my generals ship," said Yota. "Make merry my friends, though danger approaches there is still some time." "Do not let the shadows frighten you, our greatest hope is in the song of the hearts of our people." I will return shortly," said Yota. "Brock, you may accompany me, if you will." Brock stood and the two left the tent. Leappy and Gordon began talking to one another of things Alex knew nothing about. Dora, Dona and Jessica were whispering among themselves. Alex decided to look around the cave. He left the tent. The others were so busy talking they didn't notice him leave. Alex headed for the campfires but he didn't get very far when he was stopped. Two guards jumped him and took him to the ground without asking him who he was or what he was doing wandering around. The guards bound his hands. They were not at all easy about it. They took Alex to the leader of the guard. He looked at Alex and asked him what his business was wandering around the camp. "I am here with Leappy and Yota," said Alex. "Yota!" gasped the leader. "Untie him at once and escort him to the generals tent. "In times like these it is best you stay close to those you are with," said the leader. "My troops could have killed you as easily as they bound you up." Alex shook his head yes to the soldier with fear in his eyes. By the time the guards had returned him, Yota and Brock were already back. With fire in his face, Yota dismissed the guards and stared at Alex.

Yota stared into Alex's eyes so deeply and with such purpose, Alex slowly lowered his head in shame. "Enough, human," said Yota. "Hold your head up." "It is well that you know you have done wrong." "I accept your humility as a sign you are sorry." "It is for your life's sake that you do not separate yourself from this company or you surely will meet your end." "It is true that matters are terrible and the menace crawls this night as we meet here." "Brock you at my side." "Leappy, you and Gordon see the Pixies to Anton." "You may choose your own speed." "As for me, I go with the flow of the river." As Yota spoke his chest rose and his cheeks glowed red as his jaws clenched. His departing words were forced through clenched teeth. "I must pass on the report of the runner to the King and to my cousin, Prince Leroy." Yota and Brock took leave of their friends, their walk, almost at a run.

CHAPTER 12
TO WAR

By the time Alex, Leappy, Gordon and the Pixies were ready to leave, torches had been lit around the camp. The clang of armor, shields, and weapons filled the cavern. The general of this army was shouting out orders to arm and band aboard the war vessels. The Royal Youth and Alex were hastily escorted to their gondolas. As they left all they could see of Yota was his torch far ahead of them. There was little talk as Gordon and Leappy were hard at the poles. Dora did not speak at all but only stared out over the calming waters. Alex felt dread and sorrow overwhelm him. Though he didn't know the reasons for everyone's sadness, he could read the silence as a sign of the worst in times.

The two gondolas pulled up next to Yotas' already docked craft. Leappy suggested that Alex and the Pixies wait for word from the council of Chevrons at his Uncle Satchens. In the meantime trumpets sounded the summons of the Lords of the Chevrons to meet at the great Hall. Each time the trumpet sounded the citizens of Anton knew the pending war was growing closer. In the great hall the lawmakers were already seated when Prince Leroy called the council to order and to rise for the King. Anton entered the council chambers. The look of him was as majestic as his position demanded. "My Chief and most loyal friends," announced Anton. "Never in our history has there been such a need for concern, of losing our most sacred and ancient ways of life." "Not since the Queen Aurelie saw the black evil shadows approach her kingdom, was there such cause for alarm." "The Elfin Lord Yentle and Zarn, King of the dwarfs came to arms to meet that blackness." "At the cost of thousands of lives of elf and dwarf alike, even to Zarn himself was our retreat preserved to this, our underground existence." "Since the most early ages of antiquity the two brothers, sons of the race of Zarn with no fault to be found with dwarfs themselves." "Trogg and Coret have pursued to vale and extinguish the lights of Aurelies Crown Crystals." "They desire to over throw and rule in horrid evil, our people." "Trogg and Coret have grown in numbers as well as death granting power." "Their exact number and strength are not known, but we can only believe that it is enough to achieve their purpose." "My brother's son Yota, Prince Leroy and I have been in council the past half hour." "It is at my request Lord Yota, General of my armies and Admiral of my five fleets address this council." "You will grant him the same respect and loyalty as if he were I." "Yota, the Council of Chevrons is at your disposal," said Anton as he seated himself upon his throne. Beside him Prince Leroy gave Yota the salute of a warrior and seated himself at the council table with a nod to indicate his approval of his fathers choice. "Brothers of the Chevrons, it is in my despair, I address you." "Never have I been a bearer of such bad news." "For this, I am sorry," began Yota. "Less than an hour ago, I received word from a runner from the South." "Besides Trogg's slug riders and turtles, snakes and foot soldiers, he has spawned two giant brown tarantula spiders." "These awesome spiders are armed with pinchers large enough to encircle a dwarelf and crush the life out of him." "These and the combined forces of Coret are bunching together and have started the march to converge on the Twin Sisters Falls." Yota took a deep breath to calm himself in front of the Royal Court. "Coret has left his ebony tower to lead his armies." "Like his brother he has six armies." "They march along the Southern forks out of the Mole Mountains." "They are to accompany four fleets of Coratian barges and ships." "In haste, the number of turtles and snakes went uncounted." "To sandwich Corets armies of foot troops, rides five divisions of slim slugs." "Coret is not believed to have any hideous spiders." "At the speed the brothers are traveling, in two days they will join forces in the wide waste lands at the foot of the falls."

"Lords of the Chevrons," continued Yota. "My patrols will observe the blackness and keep me in constant knowledge of its progress." "I have sent messengers to our satellite cities." "I have issued orders to my Generals and fleet commanders to come to full war alert." "We have been informed in time so we won't be taken by surprise." "It had been my desire to attach first and I was put off in hopes of reasoning with Trogg." "All diplomacy was exercised to put an end to this threat." "My Lords and friends, I will now meet with my cousin Leroy and the

King to discuss methods to defend our kingdom." "It may yet be practical to be on the offensive." "Our king's approval is all I need." "I will keep you informed." "We shall be in council the rest of the night." "You may return to your homes." "Be advised to not discuss this session with anyone." "Yota snapped to attention and grabbed the hilt of his sword and bowed as he backed away from the table." Immediate conversation broke out as the King and Prince joined Yota in his retreat to chambers.

After drink was brought by servants. The King's chamber doors were closed. "Yota," said the King in a stern voice. "As a diplomat it was my duty to try and reason with Trogg and Coret." "I had no way of knowing that it wouldn't work." "I don't make excuses for my actions but only to say it is now necessary to use your military expertise and seek Aurelies blessing, that this matter be resolved for the life of our race." "True," said Yota. "I am a soldier, but I remind my King I am not without desire to have little or no lives lost and I will serve my Lord and our kind with the choices I make." "It is clear that death marches with the evil brothers." "If life must be forfeited for peace and security let it be the lives of Trogg and Coret and thier kind." "You speak with wisdom," said Prince

Leroy. "Come now, Uncle and Yota, we must discuss the future; if we have one." "We are in need of plans and the time to carry them out." They then moved around a large map table. Spread upon it was the entire Kingdom and its boundaries.

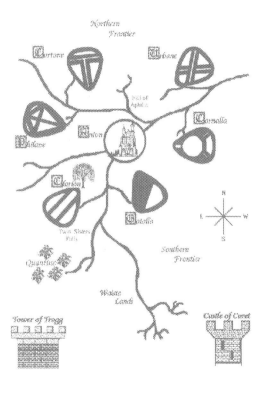

Yota began the briefing. "Though Trogg is cunning and sly, he does not move in secret." "He and Coret use sheer numbers and evil to stimulate fear among those they wish to conquer." "It is my belief they will meet and parlay on the Southern Frontier and wastelands." "If it were I, I would send most of my strength in and along the East fork of the Twin Sisters River between Clarion and Gattala." "The rest I would split half toward Clarion and the other half to Gattala." "Clarion would fall first, then Gattala." "Join forces again in the center and attack Anton." "Once Anton is captured the Center Crystal would force the rest of the Kingdom to surrender." Finished Yota. "Yes," said Prince Leroy, "I can see that would be the most probable strategy." "I too agree," said Anton. "What counter measure would you dispatch, Yota?" asked Anton. "I have thought much on this proposal. Which would be the same as if we attacked first."

"I will, within the next two hours order my fleets and armies to form a single Armada." "Taking aboard as many archers and swords as possible." "Within that time my swiftest messengers should begin to reach the knights of the King." "One great advantage for us is the Trogglites and Coretians only advance with the cool and clamminess of the dark." "During the light of day it is too warm for the slim slugs, snakes, and turtles to move." "We know nothing of the tarantulas." "We can only assume, having been bred in the swamps, they too need the moistness of night." "If I am wrong," said Yota, "it could be troublesome." "We must be prepared for the worst." "Our troops can move both by day and by night." "We need to proceed with speed." "There is yet time to spoil the plans of the enemy."

Leappy and the others waiting to hear from Yota, spoke little about the ill news from the runner at the falls of Aphilia. They tried to remain merry and were failing miserably, when a knock at Satchen's front door froze them all. Leappy answered the door and in walked Yota. Yota stood tall and straight, his jaw was locked and his eyes burned bright. Yota but stared at each member of the company. Princess Dora was the only one who looked away when his gaze met hers.

Yota spoke boldly. "This night, my friends, will be recorded in history as the gravest for Aurelie's children." "So it will, Yota," said Brock. "I am of age and wish to go with you into battle." "I too," said Gordon. "This fight, Sir Yota, is not yours alone." "This is for our families and our friends and our way of life." Ended Brock. "My friends," said Yota, "these things you say are true." "I will grant your request." "Gordon and Brock come here before me." "Kneel Brock." "I Yota, son of Yeta, knight to the king bestow upon you the title of Esquire, rise Sir Brock." "Kneel Gordon." "I Yota, son of Yeta, knight to the king dub you Esquire." "Rise, Sir Gordon." While this was going on Leappy was staring across the room at Dona. "I will also join my friends," said Leappy. "We've been together since we were elwarfs and together we played." "Now we will also fight and die if necessary for the freedom of our kind." "No!" shouted Dora, "you will not." "It is here you will stay." "Yes," said Yota, "here is your place." "You must tend to Alex and protect the pixies and citizens of Anton." "You will serve the kingdom in this role with as much honor as if on the battle field." "For this I call you before me." After Leappy was made an Esquire he rose with a strange look in his manner, a look he never showed before.

CHAPTER 13
A TURN TO THE WORST

After the trio of warriors left, Leappy, Alex, and the Pixies could but stare blankly at one another. The silence was broken when Leappy said, "Alex, Dona and I will go to the hall of chevrons and inquire of what we must do next in matters." Dora and Jessica remained at a loss for words, so Alex spoke out first. "I can not even imagine the size of your under ground world, but I feel I've come to know Yota and you fairly well enough to venture it isn't too big for them to protect its boundaries." Jessica challenged Alex's statement. "You're right. You don't know about the size of our kingdom; nor have you been here near long enough to venture anything at all about us." "Yota is gentle enough with friends, but even as close as friends as we are, we still know little about him or his clan." "He is a warrior above all else a champion." "If you thought there is little to worry about, you best consider things again." "Trogg and Coret are more evil and cunning than you, a human could understand." "That will be quite enough now, Jessica," said Dora gently. "We are all under a great deal of confusion and doubt." "That doesn't warrant taking our frustrations out on Alex, whom I'm sure meant no wrong in trying to comfort us in a time of despair." "I am sorry, Alex." "I'm sure you mean well, only," Jessica cut short what she was trying to say and began crying. "Only what?" asked Alex. Dora put her arms around Jessica's shoulder as she addressed Alex. "Only that Brock and her were to be joined together as mates on the eve of Brock's birth date." "Now he is gone," blurted Jessica, "and I'll never see him again." "Now, come, come." "That will be the end to that kind of talk." "Brock is in the best of company with Gordon and Yota." "Matters will pick up where they left off after an end to the awful events at hand." Said Dora "I am terribly sorry, Jessica, I didn't know," said Alex. "Alex, she'll be fine." Said Dora, "would you please get her a drink from the nook?"

Just as Alex was returning to the drawing room,

Dona and Leappy came through the front door. Leappy remarked. "The council is yet meeting and will be in session for the remainder of the night. Alex, I'm to take you to the hall of science." "Dona will show the Pixies to their snuggeries." "Try to get what rest you can." Ended Leappy. Alex and Leappy began their walk to the halls of science. As usual, Alex began firing questions at Leappy. "Have they found a substitute for the Quantine flower? Am I going home?" "Gee," said Alex, "I didn't mean I wanted to leave you while so much trouble was on you." "Easy, Alex, just take it easy." "I don't know what the scientist wants." "As far as you abandoning me, I accept your apology." "The trouble you speak of is not the kind of trouble any of us wouldn't be glad to avoid if at all possible." "I believe you would help in defending the children of Aureile." "You are a good companion; even for a human." Alex looked at Leappy with a frown. "Hold on, Alex." "I was only ribbing you." "I suggest light thoughts when the heart is heavy with sorrow." "If it would help you, there are some things I do know." "Such as, what else I learned from the council of Chevrons." Said Leappy. "Sure," answered Alex.

"While we were at the falls of Aphilia earlier tonight,

Yota sent runners to Cortaine, Urbane, and Phillain." "The generals and admirals of their forces were instructed to merge on Anton." "Within two days, the might of Sir Phillip, Sir Duran, and Sir Yeta will be in the bay of Anton." "Foot troops, archers, and swordsmen from Cornalla and Phillain are to reinforce Gattla and Clairion." "Even though Clairion has no citizens, it would be disastrous to let Trogg set up base for his vile creatures." "The council will put into motion emergency measures for the city." "All inhabitants will put together necessary supplies and weapons for the incoming troops." "Doctors and nurses will board the ships and barges." "After that, I have little knowledge of, but my mind runs wild with ideas."

The two reached the threshold of the Halls of Science. "Would you like for me to come in with you?" asked Leappy. "You've come this far, of course I want you to come in with me." Stated Alex. The pair entered the hall. It was in mass confusion. Doctors, nurses, and orderlies almost at a run, were shuffling from room to room, carrying arms full of medical supplies and linens. A short, round doctor motioned to Leappy and Alex to follow him. They were brought into a laboratory where three scientists and another doctor were working frantically with test tubes and chemicals of strange colors.

"Hello Alex, my name is Doctor Zoren." "I am in charge of this project." "My collaborator, Doctor Pentle, and three of his finest scientists." "We felt it an appropriate time to inform you where you stand in regard to your size." "The doctor in charge at Clarion, when the catastrophe occurred may have been wiser to have tried to shove you back through the hole you fell through than administer the milk of Quantine." "He had no way of knowing the results of his actions." "However, I in a similar circumstance, may have done the same thing, who knows?" "In any case, the amount of time it took to shrink you to your present size, is 53 times the length of time it will take for you to reach your normal height and weight." "Within six hours of your last dose of the Quantine, you will begin to feel nauseous and woozy." "Within eight hours, you will experience mild tension and aches." "In less than twelve hours severe pains in all limbs, accompanied by a strong headache." "After that I can not estimate the time, but you will under go a blackout and regain normal size, at least, normal for you." "In short, lad, you will grow out in the reverse way you shrank in." "This is mostly estimated figures since such a thing has never been brought up before." "There is enough Quantine for four more doses." "In other words, in a little more than two days the first symptoms will begin, unless the milk of the Quantine flower is administered into your blood stream." "With the war on the verge of breaking out, I haven't even an educated guess at the possibility of this." "We believe we have found an alternative." "We will first need to run some tests on you, Alex." "Leappy, will you please wait in the next room?" "These tests will not take too long." "Sure doc," said Leappy. "See you soon, Alex." "Thanks," said Alex. The doctors and scientists gave Alex a complete physical and blood work up. "We will have the results of your examination in a few hours, Alex." "You and Leappy may return home and I will send for you," said Doctor Zoren.

"Is everything okay with you, Alex?" asked Leappy. "Besides a little soreness from the needles, I'm fine," answered Alex. "We'll go home and you can get some rest." "I doubt that will be possible Leappy, but I certainly will give it a try," commented Alex.

CHAPTER 14
ALEX BECOMES A WARRIOR

When Leappy and Alex arrived at Satchens, they found Jessica and Dona were in their snuggeries and Princess Dora was waiting up for their return. "Leappy," said Dora, "I would like to go to the Tower of Anton." "Would you please escort me there?" "Alex, you know where your snuggery is." Ask Leappy. "Yes, of course," said Alex. "Lady Dora, I will take you to the tower." "Are you ready?" asked Leappy. "Yes, Leappy, I am," said Dora. Alex went to his room and tried to rest but was troubled so that tossing and turning was as much rest as he got. He sat up in his bed and gazed out the window. Shades of blue were turning to the first signs of pink. Alex found himself pondering over what new events this new day would bring. As he leaned back against the headboard, he could hear a voice in the distance. It was the voice of Dora singing from the tower of Anton. She was singing in the new day for the children of Aurelie. Her song was soft and pleasing. Alex began to drift off to sleep, with dreams of meadows and streams, the same as he did the first time he heard Dora sing at the bon-fire.

Not knowing how long he was asleep, Alex was awakened by a tug on his toes. It was Leappy. "Come now, Alex, bring yourself around." "The doctors have sent for you." Breakfast is at the table." By the time Alex reached the dining room the others had finished eating and were gathered in the parlor. Alex looked at a small vile that sat empty in front of his plate. He knew it was supposed to hold his dose of Quantine, and he stared at it with great disappointment. He only played with the food on his plate and drank his drink. Being very tired and weary he walked into the parlor and asked, "Leappy, are you ready to go? I'm in a bit of a hurry to hear what these witch doctors have to say." "Yes, I'm ready, Alex," said Leappy, "but what is a witch doctor?" "Never mind that now. Where is Dora?" asked Alex. "She is atop the Tower of Anton," said Dona. She will remain there until the danger and threat to our kind is either past or comes to an end." "I dreamed I heard her sing," said Alex. "It was no dream," injected Jessica. Leappy and Alex once again departed for the Halls of Science. Alex was even more down hearted that he was the first time. They reached the Halls of Science and Alex approached Doctor Zoren. "Slow up son." "Come in and sit down." "It is up to you if you want your companion to come in with you or not," stated Doctor Zoren. "Well, come on Leappy." "Let us get down to the business of things," said Alex. When they were all seated in the examination room, Doctor Zoren began by clearing his throat. "After several tests on your blood, we think we have found an alternative to the milk of the Quantine Flower." "I remind you though, if time allowed, I would have run a great deal more tests, but..." "But what, doctor," asked Alex. "So you noticed that I am a little hesitant." "Brace yourself young man, for what I am about to tell you will most likely be the toughest thing you've ever had to hear." Alex looked at Leappy with fear in his eyes. What could be worse than him being in the land of the Leprechauns at their worst time in history, with a war knocking at the door, thought Alex. "Give it to me doctor; all at once, if you please."

Said Alex. "You're a brave lad," said Doctor Zoren. "After deep study and all the calculation, there is no doubt the alternative medicine will keep you at your present size." "All right!" said Alex, "that's just what I needed to hear." "Hold on now, son, I'm not finished." Said the doctor. "We don't even have a name for this magic brew, nor do we know what else it could do besides keep you small." "Most of all, I don't believe you understood what I said." By taking this new serum you will remain at your present size." "Yes I understood that part, doctor." "Alex hold on tight now and listen." "You...will...remain...at...your...present...size.…forever." "What?" shouted Alex. "You're trying to tell me I could never go home again?" "No son, I'm not trying to tell you anything." "I am telling you that if we cannot get a fresh supply of Quantine you will be here for the remainder of your days." Stated the doctor. "No! No! No!" screamed Alex so loud that the hustle and bustle of the Hall of Science came to a complete stop. Leappy clamped his hands on Alex. "Easy now, Alex, take it easy." "All that anger will not change anything at all." "Let's hear what else the doctor has to say." "Thank you, Leappy," said Zoren. "I will gather my charts and present this problem back to the Council of Chevrons." "They will make any final conclusions." "If you would please wait in the hall for me, we will all go together."

When Doctor Zoren joined Leappy and Alex, they left the great Hall of Science and walked the short distance to the council of Chevrons. They remained speechless as they walked. Dora, still atop the Tower of Anton, continued to sing. Her song seemed heavy and troubled, and Alex could feel compassion for her even in his own time of trouble. They were greeted at the large doors by guards, who until this moment had no purpose to be there. "You will wait here," said one of the guards. "I will announce your arrival." The guard returned and said, "Prince Leroy would have you wait in his chambers." "He will join you there as soon as he can fit you in." The guard showed the threesome to Prince Leroy's chambers and told them cakes and ale would be sent in shortly. Alex sat quietly and looked around the large, spacious room. He seemed very interested in the paintings over the mantle of the fireplace.

Doctor Zoren, being very observant, asked Alex if he would like to know what the pictures were about. "Yes, doctor, I would. It would help keep my mind off matters some." Said Alex. Alex didn't know it but that was the intention of Doctor Zoren in the first place. "This large painting here is from memory by Sir Yentle. It is a portrait of Queen Aurelie. At her feet are some of her cherished wood nymphs." Alex could hardly believe that someone so beautiful actually existed. Here to the left is a portrait of King Zarn, the Dwarf. This painting caused Alex to look hard at the eyes of the king, who seemed to be staring at him. He had a full beard and shoulder length hair and across his lap was a gruesome looking battleaxe. "To the right of the Queen's portrait is sir Yentle." "No one, probably not even Yentle himself, knows his true age." Yentle was standing next to a great tree. He was dressed much the same as Yota. He was tall and fair complexioned and looked very much like Prince Leroy. There were several other paintings portraying the elves and dwarfs and their lives before man. Also on a wall, separate from the others, were scenes from the war with the humans that sent the children of Aurelie underground. Alex felt sad that such a free and beautiful people as the elves could be cut off from their Queen and the woods, streams, and animal friends. Alex also could sense the doctor looking at him in such a manner as to say, see what man has done. Even before the refreshments arrived Prince Leroy came to chambers.

"What news of the human, I mean news about Alex have you, Doctor Zoren?" When Doctor Zoren told Prince Leroy of his findings and solution. It hit Alex as hard as the first time he heard it. "Listen, Alex. We are doing what we can about you and the marching doom coming our way." "You now must search and face things inside yourself that you may never have had to face until this time." "In the event the milk of Quantine cannot be reached in time, most decision of your fate rests with you." "There are three things I believe that may take place with you." "One, you are given a fresh supply of the milk." "Two, the milk cannot be had and you take the substitute serum and remain with us for the rest of your life." "These first two alternatives are dependent on circumstance." "The third decision is mine." "I will hold my tongue until I have talked with my father and the other members of the council. In the meantime, doctor, how much Quantine is left?" asked the Prince. "Three doses, Prince Leroy," answered the doctor. "I thought so." "Okay, Leappy, you are to take Alex and join Yota at the blacksmith shop where Gordon and Brock are being fitted for breast plates, shields, and weapons." "You and Alex are hereby ordered to suite for battle." This I proclaim in the name of haste."

"Alex, you will have to go to the supply of Quantine flowers at the Twin Sisters Falls." "If there is time before the blackness reaches them." "To send a runner there and back would take more time than we have to waste." "Even if the flower could be had, your going would cut the time in half." "In the event it cannot be had, you will take the new serum with you and make your decision on the battlefield as to whether or not you will administer it to yourself." "Doctor, you are dismissed to return to your duties." Leappy, you have your assignment to fulfill." My squire will catch up with you in the course of this day." "I will send word to you when I've further talked this news over with council." "Every hour is important so be quick about what you need to do before tomorrow." "The first of the fleets and troops have been sighted approaching Anton from Philane and Cornolla." With this charge, the Prince left chambers.

CHAPTER 15
ARMOR FOR ALEX

Leappy and Alex approached the blacksmiths shop and the ring of hammers meeting anvils filled the air. "Leappy, things are happening too fast for me." Said Alex. "Fear not, friend, as I've told you before, things will work out if you only just believe they will." "Let's take care of what is in front of us at this moment and the rest will fall into place." Commented Leappy. Brock was getting on a bench and a smithy was fitting him with shin guards. Another was measuring Gordon around the chest for his breastplate. "Alex! Leappy!" said Yota, with the sound of surprise in his voice. "We've been sent here by Prince Leroy to be fitted for battle." Answered Leappy. "What?" Questioned Yota. "There is much more to being a warrior than armor." "Leappy, you should know that." "You. Maybe, but it could be more than Alex can handle." "Hold it, Yota," snapped Alex. "I do not doubt your abilities and you should not questions mine." "First of all, it's not by choice I'm coming along but as a matter of life or death." When Alex had said these words, he realized what the third choice of Prince Leroy was. He held this thought for a moment and chose not to linger on that possibility too long. He finished telling Yota, besides by person, I will fight as hard as any elfwarf or dwarelf for the protection of my friends." "Hum, I see," said Yota. "I truly believe you would." "That's the measure of courage I didn't know you had in you, Alex." "Very well then, suit up." "Leappy, I will join you in council." "When you and the others are ready, meet me under the tower of Anton by the fountain." "Bring Jessica and Dona with you." "It very well might be the last time we can all be together before the first arrow flies." "Yes, of course, Yota, as you say," remarked Leappy.

The blacksmith shop was smelly and dirty but Alex's mind was turning around so much he hardly noticed. He was the first to be completely suited. Gordon, and Brock were busy trying battleaxes. When it came to a weapon for Leappy he chose the bow and arrow while Alex took up a sword and dagger. The four new warriors left the blacksmith shop and headed for Uncle Satchen's abode. When Jessica laid eyes on Brock, here tears began to flow again. This time Brock was there to comfort her. "Dona, would you please help Jessica in the nook and bring food and drink to the table?" asked Leappy. Dona spoke up first. "Leappy, what is the meaning of this?" "Of what?" asked Leappy. "When Yota said you were to remain here with me I felt great joy." "Now I see you in the garb of a warrior." "It can only mean you too are leaving and my heart is in my throat." Then Dona began to cry. When Alex looked at Jessica he could see, she was trying very hard not to cry herself. Alex stuck out his arms and she ran to him and put her head on his shoulder and let her tears go. When Alex looked at Leappy over Jessica's shoulder, he could see a tear falling down Leappy's chin. Alex's chest swelled with feeling for his new friends, and he too felt tears come. It was Jessica who interrupted this display of emotions. "Quiet a moment and listen." A very faint plump, plump, plump was coming from outside. The company looked at one another and all ran to the door at the same time. The light was fading into blue, meaning nightfall would come soon. They listened in the direction of the thuds and Leappy said, "Look, torches!" "They are coming down both forks of the river." "It must be the warships of Philane and Cornalla." "They are approaching the upper bay of Anton." Without even closing the front door, they ran to the river banks as the beating of war drums grew louder. When Leappy and his friends reached the upper bay the sounds changed from plump, plump, to plump, swish, plump, swish, plump, swish. It was a ponder hammering out cadence for the oarsmen. The lines of barges and ships looked unending. As the fleets pulled into shore and lay anchor in the bay the youths were joined by, Yota. "Listen, Leappy, you all must meet at the tower in one hour." "I will try and be there by then." "I must first meet with the generals and admirals of this fleet to give them a briefing and formulate my plans for an armada." Leappy knew, at that time, Yotas' responsibilities would not allow Yota to be at the final gathering of the Royal Youth. Just the same, Leappy said, "you can count on it Yota." "Thanks, Leappy, may the Queen's love be with us all," was Yota's parting words.

"Brock," said Leappy, "you and Gordon fetch a keg

and the rest of us will bring something to eat." "We will meet you at the Tower of Anton." With these directions, the company split and went their separate ways. As the rest of that day had gone, the hour passed quickly. Brock and Gordon were already at the Tower when Leappy and the rest showed up. They were sitting on an iron glad bench drinking a schooner of ale and listening to the songs of Princess Dora. Leappy and Dona pulled up another bench and sat down. Jessica and Brock spread a quilt and sat. Only Alex was left, standing and looking upward toward the tower of Anton. "Alex," said Gordon, "you've come a very long way with us in such a short time." "We know very little of your kind but I must say, if the rest are anything like you, our elders have been mistaken for a very long time." "No, Gordon, all my kind as you say, are not like me." "Even here in the Kingdom of Anton, you have good and evil." "So it is in my world." "If you will please forgive me, I am trying very hard not to think about back home." Alex hung his head and turned from the others as to hide his feelings. Gordon stood and put his hand out to Alex. Alex looked up at him and took his hand. Gordon then pulled him to the blanket and wrestled around with him for a moment. "Come now, my friend, let's be of free spirits while we can for tomorrow we may die." This sentence froze Gordon himself when he had thought about what he had said. Leappy and Dona stood and began to stroll along the riverbank. In silence, Jessica and Gordon, along with Brock, began to wander towards the bay. Alex was trying to hold his chin up as grandfather McNaire would say, without having much success. He heard Princess Dora from atop the tower. He looked up and the Princess was looking down at him. "Alex, I've not said this to anyone before." "My heart is troubled for you." "I wish the best in all that affects you." "You must know I would have you to stay if it were up to me." "These feelings may come from all the confusion around me, I don't know, but I knew I must at least tell you." "Maybe it's because I wish to see the sky, the stars, and other wonders of your world that I am drawn to you." "I have something here I wish you to have before you leave." Dora leaned over the rail of the tower and let go of something shiny. It fell at Alex's feet. When he picked it up he heard Dora say, "keep this and remember me." Dora then again began to sing. A messenger came into the park and yelled for Leappy. Leappy and the rest came running, with Leappy shouting, "What! What is it?" The runner gasped for his breath. "Lord Yota wishes your presence, along with those of Brock, Gordon, and Alex."

"Yes, of course. Return at once and announce we are on our way," Leappy said.

CHAPTER 16
THE FLEET IS LAUNCHED

Alex didn't know at that time what Dora had given him. He just clinched his fist and stuck it in his pocket and hurried down the walk with the others. The guards at the door to the Hall of Chevrons came to attention and let the band pass. The huge doors were swung open. Alex could see the throne with Anton sitting upon it. From behind the King stood Prince Leroy and Yota. Prince Leroy motioned for the young warriors to enter the council hall.

The King was addressing his audience. "It is a horrid thing that crawls toward us this night." "Though Trogg and Coret march with death at their side, we have advantages in strategy." "I would not be a good Lord if I did not tell you to look at each other." "To your left and to your right in front and behind one another." "Out of the faces you see, not all will live to see their homes again." "With the love of Aurelie I pray it is not many." "My son and Yota are my ambassadors. I am sorry I will not be beside my siege in battle." "I will now take leave of you and go to the tower of Anton and listen to the songs of Princess Dora." As the King stood the host of warriors snapped to, with one single motion. This startled Alex who too took his sword by the handle in reverence to the King.

"My brethren and fellow warriors I have received word that our plight is even worse than we first estimated." "From atop the Twin Sisters Falls our scouts have observed Coret and Troggs camps are preparing their advance to converge in the Southern Plains." "It has also been reported that hideous spiders breed for war, carrying death in their jaws, are not effected by the light of day." "It is my guess that Trogg will use these spiders as the first line of offense to attack Clarion and Gatalla." "The two forks off the Twin Sisters River are full of foul snakes and hull crushing turtles." "They are advancing to meet at the main river." "Clarion and Gatalla have fortified their Southern walls with all available warriors." "Their fleets are on the upper stem of the river headed for the falls." "Reinforcement has been dispatched at my order from Cornalla and Philane." "These reinforcements will not reach the cities before death strikes its' first blow." "There is no time to parlay." "You will listen an act upon my word." "Admirals, you will order your crews and oars to shore." "There they will put out pallets and catch what sleep they may." "Generals you will order your warriors to load and supply the barges and ships." "Take only what is needed." "When the loading is completed you will let your wards sleep aboard ship." "Fresh oars will be boarded to put their backs hard to it and be on the way." "Are these orders received and understood?" Ask Yota. A roar of "YES SIR YOTA" came from the floor of the great hall. "Prince Leroy will lead you out of the bay at first chance." "I and my fleets and armies will leave within the hour." "Good luck and may the love of Aurelie be with us all." Ended Yota.

As soon as Yota finished, the hall began to empty. Leappy, Brock, Gordon, and Alex pushed their way to the front and came to Yota and Prince Leroy. "Brock, Gordon, and Leappy my close and dear friends it is time for you to say goodbye to your pixies." "Be quick about it and return to the docks when you are finished." "Leappy, you and Alex will be with me on the lead barge." "Gordon, to the Bow-ship to the right and Brock to the one on the left flank." "Be off now and make haste." "Alex, come with me." "The doctor has left this vile for you." "Keep it safe from harm, your life may depend on it." "Now I will tell you of your third and last choice." "If we can not retrieve the milk of Quantine and you refuse to administer this serum." "I have ordered you put to death." "Yes, Yota I thought that was it." Said Alex. "Alex I have no dislike for you, but for the sake of the damage your growing would cause to my people and our world, it must be so." "Yes, Yota I understand." Replied Alex. "Very good then." "Let's go after the milk of Quatine and put an end to those evil black hearted brothers." Finished Yota. Alex wasn't as all fired anxious as Yota but it was what needed to be done. Alexs' father Michael would have said, let's be done with it as to go on to something a bit more enjoyable.

Alex and Yota made their way out of the hall of Chevrons, down a path to Yotas gondola. As they stepped onto the boat Yota took off the pouch on his arm. "Here Alex keep your vile in this." "Perhaps you'll be able to return it some day," said Yota. "My fleet is in the lower bay." The two remained quite. The gondola slid in along side the barge. As soon as Yota climbed the rope ladder and his foot hit the deck of the barge, he started to shout. "Light the torches and weigh anchor." One by one torches began to glow. From their light only a small portion of the shore could be seen, only enough to guide the ships. Alex almost jumped overboard when the ponder started in. "Relax Alex it will be late morning when we first see the Twin Sisters Falls." Like at the time of the storm, Alex felt helpless and terrified. It hit him hard that he was speeding towards a foe, which dealt in death. He wanted at that time to jump and run. Where could I go? Thought Alex. He leaned back braced against the anchor ropes and shut his eyes. The constant pounding kept him from sleep, but somewhere in the middle of the night he found rest.

As morning came around so did Alex. The first faint light of day was blocked by fog. There was also a smell that was awful to the nose. "Here human child" said a raspy, deep voice. "Drink this." Alex looked up to the most ugly face he'd ever seen. It was covered with deep wrinkles and was scared. To beady little eyes gave the only indication that it was a face at all. "What is that awful smell?" Asked Alex. "It's on the breeze lad coming from just where we're heading." The voice of Yota intruded. "It is unusual to smell the foil odder of Trogg this far North." "One should remember Trogg is probably, farther North, than he has been since he was driven out of the kingdom, many, many ages ago." "Be thankful for the fog though; it will aid in our arrival at the falls." "If you listen closely enough you can hear them already." Said Yota. The Admiral aboard Yotas' barge said. "Sir Yota, we have just passed the Clarion outpost branch." "Good Admiral signle the fleet to disburse at the Clarion/Gatalla forks of the river." "Half to the left, the other to the right." "This barge and the first two bow ships will stay with us on to the falls." "Yes, as you say Sir Yota," answered the Admiral. As Yotas barge moved down river and the others split up towards Clarion and Gatalla, the fog began to lift. Yotas barge steered to shore and dropped anchor, as did the two bow-ships. "Alright warriors let's unload these vessels and set up camp." "Send word to the two bow-ships that I want a runner from each to scout out further down stream and report back to me at once." Ordered Yota.

While Yota was busy sitting up headquarters, Alex sticking close to the camp walked off on his own. He was kicking pebbles when he caught drift of that awful foul smell. It was even stronger than aboard ship. He bent down and picked up some stones and started throwing them into a bunch of bushes. A terrible screech came from the bushes and up jumped a what ever thought Alex. It had the face of a wolf, a tail of a horse, arms, legs, and body covered with black hair. It looked at Alex and showed its crooked yellow teeth. It turned and started running in the opposite direction. Alex began to yell at the top of his lungs, "YOOTAA!" Yota was almost to Alex when he saw the beast. He swiftly and in one continuous motion plucked an arrow from his quiver and placed it into his bow. He drew back and the arrow whistled and came to a stop with a thud in the center of the beast back. "Oh my," said Alex, "I'm so sorry Yota". Yota said "sorry for what Alex." "That was a warrior of the enemy." "No, Yota not sorry for him, but for straying off on my own." Said Alex "I will not tell you that that wasn't a dangerous thing to do Alex." "However it was a good thing you found him or he would have reported our landing and our surprise would have been ruined." "You've given us a few extra hours to prepare." "Come along now, you can help set up." Stated Yota. Alex had a grin on his face as the two walked back to camp.

The unloading was going along rapidly and the fog

had burned off completely. The cavern was filled with a light pink hue and was turning almost white. Yotas tent was setup and supplied. Immediately Yota sent for his three generals. They came and entered the tent. They had snapped to attention before Alex even knew they were there.

"You may go Alex but stay aboard my barge or within the camp." Said Yota. "Yes Yota," said Alex as he excused himself. The conversation started before the flaps of the tent fell closed. Alex felt some relief, at least they were at the falls and the flower of Quantine was close at hand. While Alex was in the camp he saw runners come, go into the tent and leave as fast as they came. One of the generals stuck his head out of the tent and motioned for Alex to come back in. "Alex there is no reason that you shouldn't know what is going on around you." One of Troggs spiders is at this moment attacking Gatalla." "The reinforcements from Cornolla have not arrived." "It seems at least for now they are holding it at bay." "Clarion is also under attack by a spider, reinforcements from Philane have not arrived." "My ships and barges are still a few hours from reaching these two cities under seige." "I fear if I and the three armies here with me do not cut across land, Clarion will fall to Trogg." "Gatalla will be reached before the cover of night allows Coret to advance on it." "My barges are armed with fire and cantipults." "I can only hope these will discourage the spiders and make them flee." "If not to totally destroy them." Said Yota. Alex clinched his jaw and looked Yota right in the eye. "Have you forgotten why I am here at all Yota?" "Tell me where the Quantine is and I'll fetch it myself." "Silence" shouted Yota. "Human child you are under a great deal of stress and I do understand your circumstances." "You are best to be advised." "You'll have no need of the Quantine nor the air to breath if you ever become smart mouthed with me again." "Do you understand?" Snapped Yota. Even the generals looked up at Yota. "Alex I do not apologize for what I've said." "However the manner in which I've said it was a bit too strong even for me." "In any case the Quantine is below the falls and we are above them." "There is very little hope of getting to it, if that spy moved as freely as he did this far up river." "It looks very likely the fields and Southern Frontier have already fallen under Troggs footstep." "I will send out a scout to see if it is at all possible." "I will have him catch up to us and bring what ever possible with him." "Thank you Sir Yota." Replied Alex. "Send in the three admirals of my ships." Ordered Yota. Alex sat down on a cot. The worry had begun to show on his face and he felt unusually tired. He drifted off to the fields of Aurelie. He was awakened by Yotas voice telling the admirals to arm their rowers. "I know they are not warriors," said Yota, "their sheer number may put off an attack by any patrol sent out by Trogg."

In a speedy and orderly fashion, the three armies assembled in the fields above the Twin Sisters Falls. The flags of Yeta were sent out first from the center the remaining two armies left at the same moment forming a wedge. The march was long, hot and if there was any enemy about they stayed hidden. Most of the day was spent marching before Yota called for a five-minute break. It was just enough time for Alex to sit down and realize how tired he was. Yota came to him, "well friend how are you doing." "Tired but I believe I'll make it the rest of the way." Without being asked Yota said, "there is no news from my runner yet about the Quantine Alex." "Be brave, he will show up." The armies stood and proceeded toward Clarion. The standard of Yeta was soon held high in the air. This was a signal for the soldiers to stop. As soon as the troops came to a complete stop, the most unreal screeching could be heard. The soldiers looked in awe at one another, never had anything so awful been heard before. The standard was raised again and put into a circular motion. This meant for the right flank to circle right and the left flank to circle left. Yota went straight up the middle. When the city of Clarion came into sight so did the source of the awful screeching. Alex couldn't believe what he saw. The giant spider was tearing at the walls trying to bring them down so it could climb over them and down into the city. Archers atop the battle tower of Clarion were shooting arrows at the beast as fast as they could reload their bows. On the most part the arrows just bounced off and those that did stick had little effect on the spider. Yota may or may not of known an awful lot about spiders, but he did know strategy and that would be his defense against the invader. He wanted to allow his left and right flanks to circle and enter the city from the East and West. He spread his army out in a straight line. Then having the odd numbered warriors take two steps out and ordered them all to kneel in the knee high grass. "It is my intention" said Yota "that my two reinforcement armies fight the spider from within the cities walls." "We will wait here for the barges to come up the East fork of the Twin Sisters River." "If the spider tries to retreat we will try to slow it." That all sounded well enough like a good plan but Alex felt if that ugly thing starts coming this way he wanted a head start in the same direction.

The battle raged on and the screams from the walls of Clarion ever few minutes told Yota that the weapon of Trogg was killing his warriors. Yota wasn't sure how long the fighting took place before the first of his barges dropped anchor in the harbor of Clarion but it seemed a very long while. As was the entire day, filled with so much pain and anger that time was not important enough for them to worry about. There was already enough for them to worry about. The fires were lit under the smudge pots and the tar began to steam and boil. The first flaming rocks were shot off the mark. The catapults were adjusted and fired again. Still they missed but this time they had drawn the attention of the monster. The spider put its' eight legs on the ground, hopped in jerks in a complete circle. As it rotated Yota ordered his troops to get down. He also did not want that evil thing to charge him on open ground. As quickly as it had come down the spider stood on its hind pair of legs and grabbed hold of the wall. It was almost able to pull itself up and over. Swords and spears were jabbed at the spiders' underside forcing it to let go of its hold. It screeched and fell to its back. The archers showered arrows at its belly. The Tarantula sprang to its legs headed away from the wall to the Southwest.

"Hurry," yelled Yota, "to Clarion, to Clarion." At last his three armies were inside the city. The light was turning into a light blue. Alex shook his head wandering where had the day gone. He looked around him in horror at the damage the spider had done. Bodies were being placed side by side for identification. Alex just hung his head and wept. The fires from the barges outside the wall were being put out. Yota then called his generals together. After the assignments were given and the night approached Alex knew that day would be nothing compared to the night ahead.

CHAPTER 17
THE BATTLE FOR CLARION

The mess the spider had caused was being cleaned up. The huge stones it had torn down were being put back in place. The towers were being restocked with arrows. While Alex was in the courtyard he saw a runner come in the gates and report to Yota. He really wanted to interrupt the briefing but remembered Yotas words on being disrespectful, so he just waited. From the center of those gathered around Yota Alex could see the gallant leader shake his head. Alex was called to the meeting.

"Alex we have gravely underestimated Trogg and Coret." "The spider at Gatalla was only a diversion." "The attack at Gatalla has been repelled." "However, the spider is headed to the Southeast." "The spider here headed to the Southwest." "My guess is they are headed toward their black hearted masters." "Runner find Brock aboard the barge in the bay and send him to me." Ordered Yota. "Yes Sir Yota, as you say." Said the runner. "General I want you to send two messengers." "They are to leave at the same time with the same message." "To Prince Leroy." "It is as follows." "Send your Armada down the South Fork of the Twin Sisters River." "Stagger bow-ship to barge." "Have the armies of Sir Phillip and Sir Duran surround the perimeter of Anton." "In a semi-circle, on the southern border place two re-enforced companies of archers." "Good-luck and may the love of Aurelie be with us all." "Dispatch this at once." Said Yota. "As you say Sir Yota." Answered the General. "Alex I'm sorry but there is yet no word from the scout I sent South of the falls." My warriors are brave and dependable." "I'm sure we will hear something soon." "In the meantime I suggest you eat and administer your last dose of Quantine." Said Yota. "Sure Yota, I quess." Answered Alex. "Just be strong Alex and believe, deeply believe it will happen and it will."

While Alex was finishing his meal of tough chewing rations Brock appeared and sat down next to him. "Man, am I glad to see you Brock." "Hold on Alex what do you

mean when you say man." Ask Brock. "I'm a dwarelf."
"Yes, yes so you are." Said Alex. "How do things go with
you Alex?" Ask Brock. "As well as can be expected under
such times Brock." "How about with yourself?" Ask Alex.
"Yes the same as you say, my friend, just the same." Said
Brock. While the two were talking it had just occurred
to Alex by taking the last doze of Quantine he either had
twelve hours to take more or drink the serum of Doctor
Zoren or die. "Brock I'm scared." said Alex. "Listen Alex."
Then Brock bent over and whispered in Alexs' ear. "I'm
scared too, and if it be known I think Yota has some fear."
"I hope for your sake that the right choices will be made
for you." "It's time for us to draw our duty assignments,"
said Brock. As they pulled their assignments from a bucket
sitting on Yotas' table they were pleased to be assigned the
same company. They walked to the commander in charge
of that company together. They were put on the West wall
of Clarion. If any place at all in Clarion, would seem the
least likely to fall. The light grew dim and the first signs
of torches being lit was aboard the vessels above the falls.
Soon the ships and barges along both forks of the river
shown flickering. As Alex looked out over the open fields
he couldn't see any danger headed for Clarion. Then just

outside the edge of light from their torches he thought he could see eyes staring out of the blackness of night. In deed he had, "their coming" yelled several voices at the same time. Hundreds and hundreds of the black vile creatures broke into the light. They were armed with knives and hatchets. Their teeth looked to be weapons of pain. They howled like jackals. The numbers approached Clarion as if a stew had been burnt and poured out over the fields. Slim slugs the size of which Alex had never seen caring wicked warriors at a slow but steady speed. Screams began coming from the river. As Alex looked toward the river he could see blank spots in the lines of vessels. Turtles were sinking the barges and ships. The snakes and the jaws from the gruesome shelled turtles were striking and devouring the warriors of Anton. As Alex heard the screaming he had not noticed that his own life was being threatened. The black mass was heaving ladders to the walls. The sheer number of them was almost over whelming. As quickly as ladders hit the wall they were thrown outward. The enemy just kept coming. When they were able to reach the top, the fierce battle was brought to Alex and Brock. Alex was as brave as he could be, mostly out of fear then finally in anger he dealt death with his sword and dagger as the putrid smelly animals attacked him.

The sounds of war, the clashing of steel on steel and the never-ending screams of the wounded filled the night. Relentlessly hour after hour the fighting continued. As the first faint shades of pink filtered through the blackness the enemy began to with draw as slowly and as sinisterly as they had snuck up. The ladders were pulled down and away. It was with great joy and relief that Alex and Brock stumbled over the stinky dead bodies of the enemy and threw their arms around one another. "Alex, Alex" came a voice below the planks of the wall. Brock and Alex looked over the edge of the wall. It was a warrior, "Alex, Yota wants you now, hurry." The two experience warriors climbed down the ladder and reported to Yota.

"Alex I have news for you." "The scout returned some time in the night and has just given me his report." "Human child if it is at all possible this is the worst news yet." "At least for you it is the worst that could happen." Alex was completely exhausted and weak at the knees and he fainted to the ground. "Take him to my tent" ordered Yota. When Alex came around Brock and Yota were standing over him. "There you are Alex," said Brock.

"How do you fare?" "I'm alright, at least for now." "It's OK Yota I believe I catch the drift of things." Said Alex. "Yes, Alex I thought this much." "The Quantine that was not purposely covered in sluge was pulled up to the root and set on fire." "You need some time alone to think over your other two choices?" Ask Yota. "No there will be no need for that Yota," said Alex. "I still have about eight hours before the aches and pains set in." "At that time it's possible I won't need to choose." "I may die anyway, but after last night I don't feel as afraid of death as before." "If I must die it is better done by the enemy in battle than by a friend." Ended Alex. "I'm grateful to you Alex you've grown to be a fine warrior and you've done it quickly."

The parlay was broken by yells from the guard towers. "It is coming, it is coming, in the name of the Queen they are coming, two of them, two monsters." The three in the tent knew it was the spider from the day before and the other from Gattala. Yota left the tent first shouting orders to arm the walls. The attack of the spiders went much as they had previously. The barges were just too far away to be helpful. "Yota," said Alex "I have a plan." "You do?" questioned Yota. "What might that be?" quizzed Yota. "Well, began Alex since the fire can not come to the enemy." Why not take the enemy to the fire." "Come now Alex this is no time for riddles." Said Yota. "If a warrior was to draw the attention of the spiders and made them take chase, running towards the barges, he would bring them into catapult range." Said Alex. "Yes Alex yes that would work in the event the warrior was not caught and eaten by the ugly things." "I couldn't order any of my warriors to take such a risk." Stated Yota. "You won't have to Yota, I will go." "What would you want to do that for?" "You and Prince Leroy said it would be my choice." With this Alex reach to his belt and untied the pouch Yota had given him. He held it up and shook it in front of Yotas face. The tinkle of broken glass answered Yotas question. "In the name of Aurelie I am sorry," said Brock. "I too am sorry Alex," said Yota. "Take it easy you two I still have a few hours to see a miracle." "Yota you told me as did my good friend Leappy. That if I just believe, things would always work out." "Besides I intend on making it to the barges." Finished Alex.

"Is this your choice?" Ask Yota. "Yes, it is," said Alex. "So it will be as you say Alex." Again it is a shame that all humans are not as you Alex." Said Yota. "Wait, hold on Yota don't make me out to be a hero until the spiders are destroyed." Said Alex. "Yota, Brock spoke out." "There are two spiders and so there should be two running bates." "I want to go as a matter of my choice." Brock my very dear friend, if you wish it, so it will be as you say." Answered Yota.

The hissing of the spiders were loud and grew more so as Brock and Alex left the city gates of Clarion. Alex began throwing stones at the closest spider while Brock began to empty his quiver of arrows in the other. It didn't take much couching to draw the spiders' attention. Trogg most likely kept them near starvation to keep them hungry enough to be vicious. That they were and not at all pleased that supper was throwing rocks and shooting arrows at them. The spiders dropped all their legs to the ground. With only a few strides they were on the heels of Alex and Brock. "Maybe this wasn't such a good idea!" yelled Alex to Brock. Brock paid absolutely no attention to his companion. The race for the barges was on. The air was already filled with flaming tarred stones. Alex had to begin dodging stones in front of him as well as watching the pinchers of the hungry spider at the same time. To stop would be fatal but when Alex saw Brock fall and the spider pick him up in its vise like jaws, he began screaming and running towards Brock. Before he could reach his friend a fireball hit its mark. The spider held on tighter and tighter until Brock lay lifeless in its jaws. When Alex looked behind him the spider chasing him was reaching its pinchers for him. It was so close Alex could smell the stench of its breath. The big pinchers began to close as it picked him up from the ground. Three balls of fire hit the spider and Alex could smell the burning hair of the awful creature. With a screech that almost deafened Alex the spider flung its head back and let go of Alex. Alex sailed through the air and landed on an outcrop of rocks. He was loosing consciousness when his head began to spin and his eyes began to blur. He could barely make out the smoldering lump of the spiders carcass. Then he was out. Not knowing how long he was under Alex started coming around. He felt the cool of a rag on his forehead and a cup being pressed to his lips. A voice was telling him to drink. As his eyes began to open still blurry from the fall he could still see the smoldering spider. As he drank and his head began to clear he shook his head and rubbed his eyes.

It wasn't a dead spider that he was seeing smolder, it was his knap tree split down the middle and smoldering. As his eyes met Michaels the boys' mouth feel open. "Hey now lad, close your jaw some before it falls off." Said his father. He began to sit up and look around. "Now what is this lad that your holding in you wee hand?" "Let me see," said grandfather McNaire. Alex was holding Yotas leather pouch. When Grandfather McNaire opened it, out poured something shinny. Alex reached in his pocket to find his gift from Dora gone. "By Jobe" said Grandfather "it's gold." "A gold Deplume." "Where on earth did you come by this son?" Ask Michael. As Alex started to speak, Thomas' voice broke in with excitement. "Father look, look here in the tree." Thomas picked up a white kerchief and brought it over to where Alex was still laying. Thomas bent down and spread the kerchief out to reveal 19 more gold Deplumes. "It's a bloody Kings ransom. Spit out Grandfather McNaire. "Finding the lad in one piece is worth even more." "Grandfather winked his eye at Alex and smiled, at that moment Alex knew he didn't have to try and explain. Grandfather knew, and that was all that was necessary for Alex. Besides the gold, Leappy had given him back his white kerchief once again.

THE END

Look for Book Two (RETURN TO ANTON)